Christopher de Vinck

THINGS
THAT
MATTER
MOST

Essays on Home, Friendship, and Love

PARACLETE PRESS

BREWSTER, MASSACHUSETTS

2022 First Printing

Things that Matter Most: Essays on Home, Friendship, and Love

Copyright © 2022 by Christopher de Vinck

ISBN 978-1-64060-738-5

The Paraclete Press name and logo are trademarks of Paraclete Press.

Library of Congress Cataloging-in-Publication Data
Names: De Vinck, Christopher, 1951- author.
Title: Things that matter most : essays on home, friendship, and love /
  Christopher de Vinck.
Description: Brewster, Massachusetts : Paraclete Press, 2022. | Summary:
  "Essays that give us back the eyes of a child, the fresh vision of
  delight, and a reminder that we are surrounded with awe that we often
  take for granted"-- Provided by publisher.
Identifiers: LCCN 2022019676 (print) | LCCN 2022019677 (ebook) | ISBN
  9781640607385 | ISBN 9781640607392 (epub) | ISBN 9781640607408 (pdf)
Subjects: LCSH: Christian life--Catholic authors. | BISAC: RELIGION /
  Inspirational | FICTION / Family Life / General
Classification: LCC BX2350.3 .D397 2022 (print) | LCC BX2350.3 (ebook) |
  DDC 248.4/82--dc23/eng/20220613
LC record available at https://lccn.loc.gov/2022019676
LC ebook record available at https://lccn.loc.gov/2022019677

10 9 8 7 6 5 4 3 2 1

Cover design: Paraclete Design

Published by Paraclete Press
Brewster, Massachusetts
www.paracletepress.com

Printed in the United States of America

CONTENTS

Part Three
THE WISDOM OF HUMILITY

Part Four
WHERE IS LONG AGO?

Part Five
ORDINARY AND EXTRAORDINARY

FOREWORD

O n an August night in the first years of a pandemic that seemed as if it would never end, my wife and I finally left our home after months of being locked down and drove to the rural farm of a family member who lived four hours away. As we walked on that hot August night along a black-topped country road in the darkness of the Indiana skies devoid of light pollution I have come to know in my Chicago-area home, fireflies filled the meadow on one side of the road and the woodlands on the other, sparkling, shining, and beckoning as they lit up the sky with their yellow-green pulsing, silent rhythms.

We continued to walk in quiet, peering left and then right as the fireflies seemingly said to us, "there is light in this darkness!" It was a mesmerizing show put on by the natural world in a way I'd never seen before—or, at least, not as an adult. I am prone to melancholy, to seeing the glass half empty. That night, my cup was overflowing with joy as I walked and watched.

The wonder of childhood, running after fireflies with a Ball jar in hand, holes poked in the lid, came to me as if it were yesterday and not five and a half decades ago, and it was strangely comforting. In my mind, I began to hum a Paul Simon song from childhood that spoke about fireflies flashing and everything being all right, so I could close my weary eyes and rest. It was a good, and true, and beautiful, and sustaining moment.

Just like reading the work of Christopher de Vinck.

I first encountered de Vinck's artistry with words in my years as a bookseller when his seminal early book titled *The Power of the Powerless*, a richly detailed narrative of his relationship with his brother Oliver, was published in 1988. I have followed his work ever since through books with titles such as *The Book of Moonlight*, *Threads of Paradise*, *Simple Wonders*, *Love's Harvest*, and *Moments of Grace* that each, in their own way, offer reassurance of the goodness of God and the presence of light and hope, of joy and wonder in the world. Each of them, like the fireflies on that hot August night, say to readers, "there is a light in the darkness! There is Good. There is God."

In his classic book *The Little Prince*, Antoine de Saint-Exupéry famously suggested that "it is only with the heart that one can see rightly; what is essential is invisible to the eye." With the elegance of a poet, the wonder of childlike eyes, and the discipline of one who steadfastly pays attention to the world around *and* within him, Christopher de Vinck's *Things That Matter Most* helps us see with our hearts—to see rightly—those things that are essential to a life well-lived: a place to truly call home, friends who sustain and nurture one another, and the love of a God who knows us as children of great worth.

—JEFF CROSBY,
author of *The Language of the Soul*

INTRODUCTION

T he phrase *Kyrie eleison* is translated from the Greek "Lord have
mercy," words infused in the liturgy of most Christian religious
ceremonies, a petition to God for his guidance and empathy.

If you combine guidance with empathy, you have the liturgy of love.

What did Christ want? *"A new command I give you: Love one another.
As I have loved you, so you must love one another"* (John 13:34).

What matters most in our world of sorrow and chaos? The joy and
stability of love.

We are not born with innate mechanisms of love. We are taught that
love is the heritage that matters most from generation to generation.

My mother, my greatest teacher, the poet Catherine de Vinck,
wrote one of her most well-known poems when I was fifteen years old
in the house where I grew up, the house of poetry, the house of my
blind and disabled brother, the house where my sisters and brothers
and I jumped into the garden looking for salamanders, climbed the
trees in the woods, attempted to sell lilacs on the sidewalk:

> Love: a basket of bread
> From which to eat
> For years to come:
> Good loaves, fragrant and warm,
> Miraculously multiplied:
> The basket never empty,
> The bread never stale.

What matters most is the fragrance and warmth of love, and we learn love from inside our homes, and from our friends outside the home where such love is miraculously multiplied.

Whenever I spoke with Fred Rogers about an angry person, or a hateful person, he would say in his quiet, recognizable voice of wisdom, "Chris, he probably didn't have a mother who loved him."

When I was a boy my mother bought a record album, *Missa Luba* (passion-song). They were songs for the African Latin Mass composed by Father Guido Haazen, a Franciscan friar from Belgium. A choir of adults and children performed their rendition of *Kyrie eleison*. The harmony and mixed voices, the drumbeat, the rhythm, the passion and beauty of that song have never left me. I listened.

When I was a boy at a picnic I was sitting beside my mother under the shade of an oak tree. She was wearing a plaid skirt, and when I said how pretty the skirt looked she introduced me to the word *madras*.

"It's called madras. See the square shapes and the different colors, Christopher?" I looked.

I remember how much my mother loved the photograph of Saint Thérèse of Lisieux working side by side with other nuns doing the laundry together. "Look how they are smiling." I looked.

It is Saint Thérèse who wrote in her autobiography, "I have at last found my vocation; it is love!"

Each week, when my sister Anne and I carried our disabled brother to the bathroom for a bath, my mother walked behind us reminding us, "Be careful. Look. Don't bump Oliver's elbows on the door frame." I looked.

It was my mother, the poet, who helped me see the colors in the madras skirt, who asked me to listen to the *Kyrie eleison*. It was my mother who asked me to look at Saint Thérèse's smile in that photograph. It was through my mother's guidance and empathy as she pointed out that I learned about love, that basket of bread miraculously multiplied. "Don't bump his elbows."

Look! Fireflies illuminate the memories of the child in us.

"Christopher, here is a glass jar. Go with your sisters and brothers and catch the fireflies."

Fireflies! The glee of catching fireflies, their bodies flashing on the palms of our hands, the entire world for a few moments captured inside a glass jar.

I hope this little book can be a jar in your hands as these words flash bits of light that remind you that goodness, beauty, love, home, and friendships are lighting up what seems to be the darkness when in reality what is dark is just a pause as the fireflies pull in the morning sun for the next day that we choose to love.

I was blessed with the voice of my mother, my greatest teacher. She taught me what matters most, those little things in our lives: madras skirts, songs, photographs gathered inside the glass jar of love. We just have to go out into the garden with glee and catch that light.

Kyrie eleison. Kyrie eleison. Kyrie eleison.

—CHRISTOPHER DE VINCK
Pompton Plains, New Jersey

Part One
FIREFLIES

WHAT MATTERS MOST

Forty-five years ago I was a new high school English teacher. I looked at my very first students, wrote my name on the board, *Mr. de Vinck*, turned and laughed. The boys and girls probably thought that I was out of my mind. Then I explained that all my life Mr. de Vinck was my father. No one ever called me Mr. de Vinck, and here I was a first-year teacher with all the authority, an accredited teaching certificate, a college degree, a love of books, and affection for, well, everyone, and I was now Mr. de Vinck.

I looked at them and then I simply started waving my hand in silence, gesturing that the students stand up and follow me. They were reluctant at first. I stood at the open door, didn't speak, and waved my hand again, inviting the students to follow me. They slowly stood up and followed me down the hall, past the lockers, down the stairs to the first floor, and out into the courtyard.

I pantomimed with my hands the request to form a circle around me, and then I spoke. "I need a volunteer."

One of the many charms of being a teacher of teenagers is if you ask for a volunteer, without even saying for what purpose, many will raise their hands eagerly. Such fun.

Bernie was the first one to raise his hand, so I asked him his name and then I had a request.

"Bernie?"

"Yes, Mr. de Vinck?"

I was already getting used to that name.

"Bernie, I'd like you to make a single footprint in this bit of mud."

Without hesitation, Bernie lifted his foot, stomped into the mud, and created a perfect impression of the bottom of his sneaker. Then I spoke to the students.

"We can find the actually footprints of dinosaurs that lived millions of years ago."

My students looked at me with puzzlement.

"Seventeen thousand years ago people drew pictures of antelopes and bisons in caves in southern France."

My students were silent.

"On July 20, 1969," I explained, "the NASA astronaut Neil Armstrong created the first human footprint embedded on the moon's surface."

I looked at the faces of each student, and then I said, "Who are you?"

Then I shared with the students that in the book *Alice in Wonderland*, the Caterpillar asked Alice the same question: "Who are you?"

I said to the students that in the coming year I wanted to help them all become better readers, better writers, and better people. And then I said that Alice responded, shyly, to the Caterpillar, "I hardly know who I am, sir, just at present—at least I know who I WAS when I got up this morning, but I think I must have changed several times since then."

"One day," I said to my students, "I was just a kid, and the next I am *Mr. de Vinck* with the privilege of being your teacher this year."

I told my students that we are an accumulation of events and emotions, experiences and sensations, and we can know ourselves by looking at our own personal stories.

"Here is Bernie's footprint," I pointed. "There will never be another person like Bernie."

Bernie smiled. His friends hooted and whistled. Bernie took a bow.

"If you want to know who Bernie is," I said, "ask him about his mother and father. Ask him about his favorite food, the movies he likes, the girls he likes." More whistles and teasing.

"What we love and who we love says a lot about who we are." I told the students about a shy poet from Amherst, Massachusetts, who loved geraniums and roses. "Emily Dickinson loved to write poetry about the slant in the light, a fly, grazing grain, and she wrote about death and love, silence and eternity. She wrote about dreams and immortality. Emily left her footprint on the earth through her poems."

So I told my students that September morning that we were going to read novels, poems, plays, and throughout the year I was going to ask them if they could find themselves in these stories. "Who was your favorite person in *To Kill a Mockingbird*? Did you like Gatsby the man? What advice would you give Romeo and Juliet?"

"The stories that we read," I said, "and the stories that we live offer the places where we can discover what is essential in our lives, and where we can discover who we are. 'Who are you,' the Caterpillar asked, 'and I will be the Caterpillar all year.'" The students laughed.

"When we know who we are we can build a life upon wisdom, love, and compassion, and set the footprint of our lives firmly onto the earth for others to find who need the evidence and the inheritance of goodness as a guide for the future. When we know what matters most, we know where we are going."

I looked at the students in the courtyard, smiled, and said, "So let's get going back into the classroom and begin."

MY SPIRITUAL NEIGHBOR

It's a beautiful day in the neighborhood.
—FRED ROGERS

For eighteen years, Fred Rogers was my closest personal friend. We met at the HBO studios in New York in 1985. I was working on a research project for a company that wanted to develop a children's television program, and because Fred was coming to the city for an interview, the producers thought it would be nice if I met Fred to enhance the direction we wanted to take with our own project.

I opened a door to the "green room" and there, waiting for me by himself, was Fred on a metal folding chair. He stood up, extended his hand, and said, "I'm Fred Rogers. I'm so pleased to meet you." I thought I was going to interview Fred about the ins and outs of developing a children's television program, but when Fred said, "I am so glad to have this time to be with you," I worried that he was just being polite, and that the conversation was going to end quickly.

Our conversation lasted eighteen years. He asked me about my life and my wife and children. He reached for his wallet and shared pictures of his wife and children. We spoke about authors that we appreciated. He loved Pierre Teilhard de Chardin. "Do you know the book *The Phenomenon of Man*?" Fred asked. I shared with him one of my favorite quotes from that book: "I am not a human being enjoying a spiritual life, I am a spiritual being enjoying a human life." He looked at me and smiled. The interview was over. Fred embraced me, said how nice it was to meet me, and off he went to the cameras and lights for his taped interview.

Two weeks later my wife answered the phone at home and said there was a Mister Rogers for me. "Hello Chris, I wanted to say how much I enjoyed meeting you." I was startled, recognizing that famous voice and wondering why the famous voice was being carried over the wires and into my house. Fred asked, "Do you know May Sarton?"

"Yes, I know her work quite well. She wrote a terrific essay in the *New York Times* about solitude, and I like her poems." I shared with Fred a line from May's poem "Spring Planting": "To plant our anguish and make for it a home," and I shared that my parents, like May, were born in Belgium.

"Would you like to come to Pittsburgh and be on my program with me and May?"

A few weeks later I was sitting on the swing with Fred in his television neighborhood and speaking with him and May Sarton about writing and poetry.

After that, Fred and I spoke on the phone at least once a week, and when email was invented, we wrote back and forth every day. Somewhere along the line I asked him why he wanted to be my friend. "Chris, when I first met you in New York, you didn't want anything from me. You didn't want my autograph, you didn't want me to endorse a product or give a speech. You seemed to like me for me."

"I did like you for you."

"You know, it's hard to make genuine friends, especially when a person is on television every day."

The more time I spent with Fred, the more I realized that he was not just a friend, but a man with a deep, radical spirituality. Often, at the end of a phone conversation, Fred would say, "Well, Chris, you know who's in charge."

Often when we spoke about someone who had committed a horrid crime, Fred would say, "My guess is that he didn't have a mother who loved him."

Fred and I attended a lecture by the Vietnamese monk and peace advocate Thich Nhat Hanh. A few days later Fred mailed me a small card with this quote from the holy man: "Look at flowers, butterflies, trees, and children with the eyes of compassion. Compassion will change your life and make it wonderful."

Fred looked at us all with compassion and guided us to look closely at the flowers, butterflies, and goldfish.

It has been famously reported everywhere about one of Fred's favorite lines from the book *The Little Prince:* "That which is essential is invisible to the eye."

Fred understood the invisible, the language of poetry, the psalms of the church, and the power of prayer. He loved the book by Anne Lamott, *Bird by Bird: Some Instructions on Writing and Life*, which he gave me for my birthday one year. He underlined this quote:

If something inside of you is real, we will probably find it interesting, and it will probably be universal. So you must risk placing real emotion at the center of your work.

Fred placed real emotion and a love of God at the center of his work, and he often said that the greatest gift you can give someone is your complete honest self. For my fiftieth birthday, he gave me the gold cufflinks his father had given him for Fred's fiftieth.

We once swam together in the Atlantic Ocean off Nantucket beach. We sat together at Mass in Richmond Hill, Toronto, as Henri Nouwen spoke about compassion and goodness. I introduced Fred to Henri, and they became close friends. Nouwen, too, was a man of deep faith who struggled greatly in his loneliness and along the way wrote books that joined the voices of Thomas Merton, C. S. Lewis, and Fred Rogers in the universal need for love. Henri wrote in *Can You Drink this Cup*, "Nothing will give us so much strength as being fully known and fully loved by fellow human beings in the Name of God."

At the Mass in Toronto, Fred leaned over and whispered, "Do you hear how Henri's voice soothes us all?"

Henri needed to be loved. Fred needed to be loved. I needed to be loved, and Fred said again and again to all of us . . . we all need to be loved.

Fred was the first and only person who ever asked me, "How does God play a role in your writing, Chris?" At best I answered how much I loved the film *Chariots of Fire* and how Eric Liddell said, "I believe

God made me for a purpose, but he also made me fast. And when I run I feel his pleasure." That is what I said about writing: I do so to please God, for he made me write. Fred smiled.

One late summer afternoon Fred and I were sitting in the living room of the Crooked House, Fred's small cottage on Nantucket. We were talking about books, poetry, and writing. We laughed at the jokes we shared. I read aloud some of my poems, and then we spoke some more as the sun slowly set and disappeared. The house grew darker and darker, and yet Fred and I kept talking about our families, our joys, and our sorrows, and when it was completely dark in the house Fred laughed and said, "Doesn't God have a sense of humor shutting off the lights?"

Joanne Rogers, Fred's loving wife, and I have remained friends for all these many years. We shared in the sorrows of losing Fred to cancer. We kept in touch, telling each other about our children's progress. I once asked Joanne if she could share a story about Fred's spiritual life, about his way of seeing God's influence in the world, and she wrote me this:

Fred came home from a visit with his favorite professor from seminary, who was residing in a nursing facility during his last months. Fred loved the usual weekly visits with this remarkable friend, and this particular time Dr. Orr was thinking of the words of the well-known hymn of Martin

Luther. In one line there is mention of "the Devil" and the words say "One little word shall fell him."... And Fred was fascinated that Dr. William Orr said, "and that little word is forgiveness!" Well, that was a story that Fred took so greatly to heart, and he told it many, many times.

Fred understood forgiveness, compassion, and the love of each person he met. He saw God in all of us. Henri Nouwen wrote, "What God calls us to do we can do and do well. When we listen in silence to God's voice and speak with our friends in trust we will know what we are called to do and we will do it with a grateful heart." Fred did God's work, and he did it well.

I believe we are all Fred's children. We should remember his message, echoing Jesus: love one another. Fred Rogers: the twenty-first-century prophet in a comfortable sweater and blue sneakers.

FIREFLIES

How far that little candle throws his beams!
So shines a good deed in a weary world.
—WILLIAM SHAKESPEARE, *The Merchant of Venice*

Yesterday, at the tail end of sunset, as the orange orb was ducking out of sight, I was sitting on the deck revising a poem. "Here is the moment undisturbed with the silence of air." A summer evening is a good time to consider silence as we sit outside, inviting the forgiving cool air to replace the heat and humidity.

I like sitting on the deck as night approaches. I like seeing the last bit of sunlight disappearing from the tips of the oak trees.

After the full darkness descended, I dozed a bit on the deck chair when suddenly I felt something crawling on me. I quickly reached back, slapped my left hand onto my neck and gave it an extra swipe, making sure that whatever landed on me would not sting. When I pulled my hand back, I saw a greenish, yellowish glow on the flat of my palm, an eerie bit of light smeared on my hand. I had pulverized a firefly, and I felt awful.

Fireflies, lightning bugs, glow worms, whatever we call them, do not sting or cause harm in anyway. They seem to exist to illuminate our lives like electric bulbs at an amusement park. I like thinking about the fireflies as superheroes that move invisibly in the dark until they flash their powers in the corner of our dreams.

Fireflies glow simply to attract a mate saying, "Here I am." Their light is a beacon. Those who love ought to have a beacon, a lantern to wave above their heads to announce, "Over here, here is where I am." My wife and I live on the East Coast, and our daughter, Karen, lives just outside of Portland, Oregon, 2,838 miles away. When she calls and I hear her voice, the phone nearly glows. When I received a Father's Day card telling me that I am Karen's hero, I felt the light of the card illuminating the room.

We often come upon beacons of light that trigger hope. Think of lighthouses that seafarers used to guide them to safety, that pulsing message: *This way. This way. This way.*

Think of that famous scene in the novel *The Great Gatsby* where lonely, yearning Jay Gatsby stood on his dock and looked across the bay and saw the green, blinking light from Daisy's dock, Daisy the girl of his dreams. That green light represented hope for the future. Gatsby so much wanted Daisy to love him. That pulsating beacon from Daisy's dock across the bay was a symbol, the light of salvation flickering in the darkness of Gatsby's sorrow.

I miss my daughter. I miss finding an empty mayonnaise jar under the sink and poking holes in the lid. I miss watching Karen running in the blue, summer night and gently cupping a firefly in her small hands and shouting with glee, "Got one!" I miss sitting beside her as the two of us looked cheek to cheek at the small flashing light inside the glass jar.

We close our eyes at night like dormant creatures as memories flash into our subconscious dreams. We open our eyes in the morning and Karen, my daughter of light, is still 2,838 miles away.

Are the fireflies bits of burning grass, or the souls of the dead speaking in magic: "Here I am. Remember me. Now over here, and here, in the darkness. Remember me?"

I wonder if the fireflies ever blink in a synchronized manner, a neon message spelling out in code that we just have to find the light in our lives to endure the sorrows. Remember the famous quote: "It is better to light one candle than to curse the darkness." Eleanor Roosevelt said that. She, too, knew darkness and she knew light.

I'd like to think that we can all still catch the light of goodness in a mayonnaise jar.

BACK TO THE BEACH

Jay Gatsby's neighbor Nick Carraway said in F. Scott Fitzgerald's lyrical novel *The Great Gatsby*, "And so with the sunshine and the great bursts of leaves growing on the trees, just as things grow in fast movies, I had that familiar conviction that life was beginning over again with the summer."

We as a nation urgently feel the need for renewal, and a fresh start. We long for the normal sounds of cicadas and ice-cream trucks, for the taste of hamburgers on the grill and watermelon on our lips. We want to hold hands again and kiss and hug and go to ballgames and set up our beach umbrellas in the sand. This summer feels as if life is beginning all over again.

In this past year we closed our doors, wore masks, cancelled vacations, and abandoned routines. Even being denied our smallest pleasures drew us to a place of stress and loneliness. I couldn't play Scrabble with my mother, who was approaching her one-hundredth birthday.

Many people have died because of this world pandemic. Sorrow is an enemy all to itself. But we can regain our sense of hope when we remember we must carry on and celebrate our fortunes of life. We must remember, with love, those who have died, and we must dance, with love, with those who have survived.

Last summer I was afraid to buy any plants for the garden. This past weekend I scattered 10 trays of red and white begonias throughout the garden. I planted rhododendron bushes and grass seed. My wife bought a huge watermelon that she didn't wipe in fear of the virus sticking to the surface.

As I write I hear the neighborhood children bouncing on a trampoline. I was born on a summer day hours after my mother made a peach pie.

The summer I was ten, I read *Treasure Island* and felt Captain Long John Silver was my summer partner as I swam to the raft at our local pool and pretended it was our pirate ship. I buried silver dollars my grandfather gave me in the woods inside a metal box. I drew a map, and the following week my cat and I fought off pirates and ocean storms as we found the treasure. I liked the sound of the coins jingling in my hands.

We can once again dream of summer, pursue a romance, and visit the lakes and oceans freely and rediscover the treasures of life.

The pandemic is coming to an end. We can all, like Gatsby's neighbor, relish that there is so much fine health to be pulled down out of the young breath-giving air of summer.

Summer? A new beginning? Which way? I have a suggestion.

My grandson, Finnian, is two years old. Last weekend he had an important task. He picked up his red pail and his green shovel. He put on his baseball cap and he headed out for a Massachusetts beach. All he probably thought about was the blue water, the blue sky, and the anticipation of building a sandcastle with his mother and father.

Let's begin all over again. I think we all need to follow the boy to the summer beach.

JULY 4TH

We hold these truths to be self-evident: That all men are created equal;
that they are endowed by their Creator with certain unalienable rights;
that among these are life, liberty, and the pursuit of happiness. . . .
—THE DECLARATION OF INDEPENDENCE

In 1963, when I was twelve years old, Johnny, my best friend who lived in the brick house down the road, and I decided we were going to celebrate the Fourth of July in our own secret way.

"Chris," he said as he pulled up on his bicycle at the front steps of my house where I was waiting for him. "They're selling sparkle and bang matches at the five-and-dime store." I admired the red, white, and blue streamers he wove in the spokes of his bike.

For some inexplicable reason, Johnny and I, mere children, were able to buy these matches that, when you struck and tossed them onto the ground, they'd sparkle like a small fuse, or if you bought the other kind, they would bang like a small firecracker.

Johnny and I hid beside a small pond at the corner of a farm on July 4th and threw these lit matches at each other as we laughed and dodged until the leaves caught fire and the entire surrounding woods would have ignited if it hadn't been that the water from the pond was right there and we quickly doused the flames.

Johnny and I rode our bikes to the firehouse after we saved the world from the inferno and drank the free birch beer the firemen gave out for the holiday. One of the men behind the table leaned over and said, "Chris, how come you smell like smoke?" I sniffed the sleeve of my shirt, smiled, shrugged and then in my best Huckleberry Finn smile I asked if I could have another glass of birch beer.

On July 4, 1976, my mother and father thought it would be a nice idea to celebrate the 200th anniversary of the United States with a barbeque and games. We hung an old tire from the apple tree and created a toss-the-ball-into-the-circle game. We played horseshoes, threw Frisbees, and my grandmother, who suffered through two world wars in Belgium, held a small American flag as she sat on a lawn chair and cheered us all on. *"Vive l'Amérique!"*

I remember one 4th of July I was sick and not allowed to go to the ballpark to watch the fireworks. I sat on a dresser just to the right of an upstairs window and watched the splash of light from the highest-reaching fireworks. I wanted to be there with my family and with Johnny eating a Popsicle, smelling the aroma of cigars, and hearing the crowd gasp with delight at the flare of light and loud explosions. I liked how at the end of the show, the silhouette of George Washington and Abraham Lincoln would be illuminated in a sparkle of light and the words "good night" would equally be on display.

When George Washington retired as president he said in his farewell address, "The faults of incompetent abilities will be consigned to oblivion." Thomas Jefferson, in speaking about the rights of the British colonists who were in favor of independence, wrote, "The whole art of government consists in the art of being honest." John Adams wrote in a letter to his wife, "A Constitution of

Government once changed from Freedom, can never be restored. Liberty, once lost, is lost forever."

Each 4th of July we are reminded of our roots as a nation. Why do children weave red, white, and blue streamers into the spokes of their bicycles on the 4th? Why do we have parades and illuminate the night sky with sparkle and bang? Why do firefighters give out root beer? Why does an old woman wave a small American flag?

The novelist Ray Bradbury in his famous book *Fahrenheit 451* wrote these words:

The comfortable people want only wax moon faces, poreless, hairless, expressionless. We are living in a time when flowers are trying to live on flowers, instead of growing on good rain and black loam. Even fireworks, for all their prettiness, come from the chemistry of the earth. Yet somehow we think we can grow, feeding on flowers and fireworks, without completing the cycle back to reality.

We acknowledge the chemistry of democracy on the Fourth of July. We cycle back each year to the reality of the Declaration of Independence. We are a transparent nation, wedded to the land, and blessed with the rights of life, liberty, and the pursuit of happiness.

May we live up to these words. *Vive l'Amérique!*

INTO THE WOODS

Believe me, for I know, you will find something far greater in the woods than in books. Stones and trees will teach you that which you cannot learn from the masters.

—BERNARD OF CLAIRVAUX

The soul of a child can be nurtured inside the womb of the forest. I discovered the beginning of my small soul inside the woods behind my parents' house in search of the elusive woodcock.

The woodcock is a plump, brown bird with a long, slender beak. It is a rare bird, a bit smaller than a typical rabbit, and larger in the imagination of a ten-year-old boy.

The first time I knew of its existence was when I stood outside in the late afternoon and heard this odd beeping sound, not like a bird but more like a duck with a nasal infection. "That is a woodcock," my brother said, as he explained that he saw the bird a few days ago. "It's this big." And he gestured with his two hands, and in my imagination the bird was the size of an ostrich. I was determined to find the woodcock myself.

We human beings like answers, grope for meaning in our lives, hunt for beauty or adventure. Often the two combined create a magical elixir that stirs people to become artists or writers.

I was a lonely boy living in a vibrant home of parents and five siblings. There was enough to sustain my exterior world: a rock pool my father made for paper sailboats and summer splashing with my sister. The pine trees were young enough to climb. My grandfather walked us to town to buy ice cream cones and to feed a neighbor's horse on the way back with bits of dried grass. My sister and I played Monopoly for days in the summer until she and I were billionaires, or at least rich enough to run into the kitchen and make ourselves Kool-Aid and sit on the back porch and feel just fine.

But there was a stirring inside me, a world that I did not understand as a child, yet I knew that feeling of delight when I found it: the salamanders my brother showed me under the rocks in the woods; the glowing fungus, and the invitation of the aroma of the honeysuckle that draped itself elegantly along the barbed wire fence that divided our woods from the farmer's cow pasture.

I felt somehow protected when I was among the birch trees as I walked tenderly on the carpets of moss. I liked pretending I was Robin Hood taking a stick from the mock-orange bush and using it as my sword as I slashed my way through the wide, green ears of the low skunk cabbage while saving the poor people in Sherwood Forest from angry sheriffs and greedy kings.

I am reading the novel *Out of Africa* by the Danish writer Karen Blixen, made famous in the movie of the same name starring Robert Redford and Meryl Streep. Mrs. Blixen, also known as Isak Dinesen, said about her time as a farmer in Africa, "You know you are truly alive when you are living among lions."

Living among nature, recognizing birds, flowers, and the sound of the woodcock entice us to dream of a world deep within ourselves.

In many ways we grow alone emotionally in our private selves, cautiously taking small steps into the forest of our lives, not knowing what to expect, but if we are hopeful, we find in the deep woods of life a silence and beauty that is there for the taking when we are ready.

I never found the woodcock. They are nocturnal birds that avoid a boy on a journey and use the camouflage of their feathers to blend in with the dried leaves and brown sticks. But I loved eating wild blackberries at the edge of the woods. I relied on the love my parents gave me, that stable foundation for my adventure, and I depended on the message that waited for me in the sound of the woodcock and in the tickle of the ferns against my legs as I walked into the woods feeling free and alive as I walked among my own lions of Africa in my imagination.

I did not know as a child that what surrounded me held meaning and symbols, road signs that can guide us, but I knew how to make my way through the woods, and how to speak to the crow that often perched itself in the branch of the oak tree. "Hello, Crow," I'd say, and clap my hands, eager to watch the bird fly off, wishing that I too could join him on his way to Africa while I walked home with a feather, a stone, or a pinecone, evidence that I had discovered a small intoxication in the yielding tenderness of a nonjudgmental world.

PRECIOUS

My Precioussss!
—J. R. R. TOLKIEN, *The Hobbit*

In February 1948 my mother and father arrived in this country on the *Queen Elizabeth* from England. To them it was the new land filled with new opportunities and thoughts of a new, invigorating natural beauty, for they both enjoyed hearing about Niagara Falls, the prairies of the Midwest, the Redwood forests, and the Grand Canyon. What they didn't expect was a blue bird.

As he entered the house coming home from his new job in New York City, my father announced to my mother with gusto, "I saw a blue bird! Can you imagine! A blue bird!" My mother said it was as though my father saw an exotic creature from Tahiti or paradise. Of course, my mother dismissed this. "You must have been mistaken."

But a few days later, when my father came home once again, my mother was waiting for him to announce with her own startled voice, "Yes! I saw it. I saw the blue bird!"

Today my mother still smiles when she tells me that the extraordinary bird was just an ordinary blue jay. "There are no blue birds in Belgium, so your father and I were innocently delighted to see this exotic bird for the first time." My mother recalls that there were also no cardinals in Belgium, and they were being sold in the market in fancy cages the same way we sell imported parrots in this country.

What is rare brings delight and value: gold, a painting by Michelangelo, an Olympic medal, a Nobel Prize, the Aurora Borealis. But the true mark of a poet, or a person who lives a life of gratitude and peace, is the person who recognizes the delight and value of ordinary things: spoons, daffodils, a clock ticking, the taste of chocolate ice cream, the smile of a child. And yet one person can see the magic of a blue jay, while someone else can call that same bird a curse.

Do you remember when Atticus Finch gave his son a rifle in Harper Lee's novel, *To Kill a Mockingbird?* He said to Jem, "Shoot all the blue jays you want, if you can hit 'em, but remember it's a sin to kill a mockingbird." According to Atticus blue jays were a nuisance eating up the crops, but mockingbirds—"they don't do one thing but sing their hearts out for us."

I felt sorry for the blue jays when I read that in the book. They look like royal birds in their blue and white feathers. I read that they can live for a quarter century, they can mimic the sound of a hawk, they are among the smartest birds, and they love acorns. A part of summer for me has always had, in the background, the trill of the cicadas and the distinctive cry of the blue jay, especially when our cat was slinking through the garden.

In Tolkien's *The Lord of the Rings*, Gollum coveted that gold ring, that precious ring, that ring that could extend the bearer's life for centuries. Of course, it destroyed Gollum. What we covet as rare and precious can, in someone else's eyes, be ludicrous and destructive.

To a young couple from Belgium the ordinary blue jay was a creature created by the gods of myth and fantasy. What is precious is not what glitters, but what shines within our own hearts.

BOARD GAME

*I am convinced, the way one plays chess always reflects the player's
personality. If something defines his character,
then it will also define his way of playing.*
—VLADIMIR KRAMNIK

When I sit at my desk and wonder what I will write, or when I
pause to let something I've written stand aside for a moment,
I sometimes play chess with my computer. As I looked at the chess
pieces this morning, I was reminded how much life is like chess.

The pieces are set up on the board and placed in an agreed-upon
pattern. Before we are born, different chess pieces, different moving
parts of who we are, have to be in place and work together exactly
as they always have in order for us to inhale our first gulp of air. The
chess pieces work together. The genetic material in both the egg and
sperm mingle to create a new cell that quickly divides. Those cells
divide and then more and more cells divide, combine, grow, and nine
months later the new chess piece is born and ready to continue the
game.

When I was a child, I thought I had to choose who I was going to be
when I was born and as I grew up: a king, a queen, a pawn? But then as I
looked at the game I realized that I am all the pieces combined.

Sometimes I like being a king and dominating my surroundings. I fill
the stapler. I read the newspaper and solve the problems of the world. I

like to order the birds to flock around my bird feeder as the sun rises. (I also command the sun to rise in the morning. Kings do that.)

But I am also a queen: powerful, sensitive to my surroundings. I demand respect. I fill the stapler. I read the newspaper and solve the problems of the world. I like to order the birds to flock around my bird feeder as the sun rises. (I also command the sun to rise in the morning.) And I tolerate the stupidity of the king.

I am also a pawn. I am submissive to the power of everyone else on the board. I walk forward blindly knowing that I cannot turn back, knowing that if I act like the tortoise in the famous race I could someday be transformed into a queen. Sometimes I can step to the left or to the right of what I believe and gain an advantage. Also, if I am stubborn like that famous man who stood before the tank in Tiananmen Square, I can block an advancing attack.

I also realize that I am, at times, a bishop. I have to stick to what I believe and stick to the rules. Sometimes I express what I believe with a spurt of energy and conviction as I zoom across the board of life diagonally, never abandoning what I believe but zipping around cautiously one square at a time.

Now, the knight in me is tricky. I sometimes move in odd patterns on my horse when I am anxious. I rear up and begin to step forward, but then I change my mind and make a quick turn to my left or to my right. I am tentative and I often jump into the middle of an event or argument and wonder, "What am I doing here?"

Finally, I am sometimes like the rook, the castle. It has lots of power because it can move up and down, back and forth with great freedom. A castle is tall, proud, solid, and difficult to catch. I don't want to be caught.

Of course, it is not enough to know that different parts of me are represented by the different chess pieces. When the game of life begins, all the pieces of who I am start to move in relationship to each other, as the plants move, as the molecules and atoms move in our bodies, as the seasons move, as the guts of a pocket watch move. With all the pieces of life moving in response to the world, there is a result: the clock ticks, leaves turn yellow in the fall, our bodies expect food, sex, air, heat; the sun nourishes the earth, and the moon massages the oceans. I sit at my desk and write the next word.

At the end of our lives, once the game is played, I hope we will all be able to identify the voice that whispers, compassionately, "Checkmate."

PASSION

As if you were on fire from within.
The moon lives in the lining of your skin.
—PABLO NERUDA

This morning I woke up feeling low. The bright sunlight pouring into my bedroom like honey didn't whet my taste for the day. The sheets and pillow didn't entice me to enjoy the morning stretch of relaxation with an invitation to linger. Sometimes I wake up in the morning and feel that I cannot contain the madness any longer. I feel like a suburban Hamlet.

Hamlet's mind was filled with obsessive thoughts of sex, death, and the murder of his father. He swirled around in the play either acting like a madman to deflect his true purpose to revenge his father's death, or he was actually crazy.

We all live with this double life. We are obsessed with our interior thoughts and endure the contradictions of the exterior world. We dream about women, and men, about the next promotion, or about the blue water of the Caribbean. We swim in the lake in the summer of our minds; we climb a cherry tree in the past with our sisters and pluck the fruit with delight. And then there is the reality of the alarm clock, the bills we have to pay, the relationships that do not match our needs, the sorrows of death. It is easy to see sap oozing from a fir tree, but it is dangerous to compare ourselves to a diamond or to a beautiful seashell.

Poor Hamlet. His thoughts take him hostage. Hamlet says so himself: "Thus conscience does make cowards of us all, / And thus the native hue of resolution is sicklied o'er with the pale cast of thought."

We can look at the world in the morning and be aware of what it is that we need to do but scream with regret at the impending labor. Our resolve to tend to the battles of the day are corrupted and sickened with the illness of our thoughts. How do we balance the reality that we see with the passions that we feel?

If we were blessed to be raised in a house of love, we were promised time with the sea, under holy skies; we were given dreams of mist and fancy sailboats and beauty and goodness.

Perhaps original sin is the moment doubt was infused into the human consciousness. Hamlet hoped that his jumbled mind "would melt, thaw, and resolve itself into a dew."

How do we balance the sorrows of the body with the sorrows of the mind? How do we reconcile the physical world with the spiritual? We look at life and see all around us dust and fossils. Yes, we have moments of delight on a Florida beach and yet at night we feel life oppresses us as if the walls compress closer and closer to the final design of a coffin.

Hamlet was a pessimist. "How weary, stale, flat and unprofitable seem to me all the uses of this world." Yet, he persisted to seek an answer to his struggles. "To be or not to be, that is the question." Is it nobler to suffer the disappointments of our circumstances, or to fight such losses, to oppose our exterior selves and fight to the death the battle of our inner conflicts?

We are slaves to passion. The ghost finally asks Hamlet to save the queen from his revenge. "Step between her and her fighting soul." What or who steps between the morning and our fighting souls? The person lying next to us? The lark at the window? A morning prayer? The sound of a son or daughter in the next room?

For many people the chains of melancholy are lifted with a simple shower and a cup of coffee. Acceptance is one path to inner peace. Accepting the quiet fall of the sparrows of our passions allows us to inhale with a sigh, helps us adjust our tie or to slip on our shoes and greet the day with courage. "There is a special providence in the fall of a sparrow. If it be now, 'tis not to come; if it be not to come, it will be now; if it be not now, yet it will come. The readiness is all."

We need to be ready for the physical day. We also need to be ready with the spiritual day that wears upon us like a skin of passion. Yes, we need to greet the day with the eyes of desire, but also with the hunger for a resolution between our exterior and interior selves.

As Hamlet said, if we ignore "the heart-ache and the thousand natural shocks that flesh is heir to," if we ignore the "whips and scorns of time," if we ignore "the pangs of disprized love," we dream of pleasure. But if we recoil from the body, how may the spirit survive the hot shower in the morning.

If we do not dance with sorrow, we will not hear the banjo of joy. "Aye," Shakespeare wrote, "there's the rub."

The readiness is all.

GOOD BONES

What need the bridge much broader than the flood?
The fairest grant is the necessity.
—WILLIAM SHAKESPEARE, *Much Ado About Nothing*

What is 604 feet high, 4,760 feet long and 119 feet wide? The mighty George Washington Bridge that connects New Jersey to the city of New York.

Over 108 million cars cross the span each year, making it by far the busiest bridge in the world. The four cables that bear most of the weight of the bridge could be stretched 107,000 miles. These are known facts, but there is one fact that many people do not know. The bridge is unfinished.

The George Washington Bridge has those two famous, tall towers anchored into the bedrock with 260,000 tons of concrete. Those towers were originally designed to be covered with granite slabs, completing the final look on the engineer's drawing board, but because of the added cost, the granite was never used, and we have those exposed girders and beams in those towers adding to the famous image we all know.

What is 5 feet 10 inches high and too wide at 195 pounds? The not so mighty Chris de Vinck who tries to connect the angry, pessimistic world to optimism with cables of hope that stretch from here to eternity.

I too am unfinished, hoping to live until 100 as my father did. I feel that I am anchored in the bedrock of literature, my family and friends, held together with the cables of poetry. But unlike the famous bridge, I feel as if I am finished; the tower of me is fully covered not with granite but with the magic of our skin.

The only way that I can see the hidden girders and beams of my body is with an X-ray. Because I fell three weeks ago in Florida, because I felt jabbing pain in my right arm with each movement, I thought it best that I visit the doctor this morning. He moved both of my arms up and down. He asked me to push against his hands, checked the strength in both arms, and while he said that I had good strength, he wanted to see if anything was broken, so I had two X-rays. After a few moments, the X-rays were taken and were slipped onto an illuminated screen.

I tried to listen attentively to the doctor's words: nothing broken, an internal bruise that will heal itself in a few weeks. I tried to focus on what he was saying, but I was distracted. There they were! *My bones!*

I'd rather think that the inside of my body is made up of willow sticks and moon dust, but no, there was the proof: bones. I don't want to know about my bones. I don't want to see my bones. There they were: my humerus, scapula, and clavicle. The clavicle sounds like a musical instrument; the scapula sounds like the robes monks wear, and the humerus seems to be an adjective that describes a Las Vegas comedian.

I'd rather be made up of monk's cloth and violin strings and laugh about the humor of it all than be a collection of hard bones made of calcium and collagen.

BATHING IN THE WATERFALL

Let a little water be brought, and wash your feet,
and rest yourselves under the tree.
—GENESIS 18:4

E very time I see a waterfall I want to strip and stand under the cascading rush of foam and water and bathe in the cold gift from the hills. Is there anything more sensual than bathing in a waterfall? I've never done it, but it seems like something we all ought to do.

Frederic Edwin Church, known as being one of the Hudson River School of American landscape painters in the early 1900s, painted many waterfalls. He created wild, cascading scenes that were realistic and yet at the same time magical and majestic, expressing a sense of optimism that was part of the early American spirit. His paintings express a beauty that gives us an elevated feeling as we stand before a grand scene of nature, the same feeling we get when we stand on an ocean shore and look out toward the powerful expansion of water, motion, and mystery.

We need to feel elevated. We need to feel that we are a part of something larger than ourselves, for it gives us a feeling that we too belong to the grand plan of existence.

I have been to Niagara Falls. The peak flow over Horseshoe Falls was recorded at 225,000 cubic feet. I do not even know what that means, but it sounds like a lot of water. I remember the roar of the falls as I stood at the rim. I remember the huge spray and the wild movements. It seemed as if someone had cut open the seam of the ocean and it was gushing out in one violent, life-draining action. The power of nature has no equal.

I often feel a wave of gratitude for my shower in the morning: the hot water pressing against my face and rolling against my cheeks; the water massaging the aches out of my back and shoulders. I listen to the water splashing. I inhale the aroma of the soap. I can understand why people sing in the shower. I don't. I am no Gene Kelly and wasn't meant to be. I sing in the silence of poetry. I sing with words and hope that those who read my work hear the music of my sorrows and joys. I hope my words splash against the faces of the readers, massaging the aches and pains from their backs and shoulders.

I don't express the power of the waterfall as painters do as they stand before the rugged scene and recreate on a canvas its beauty and its glory. I wish I could paint a waterfall and carry the picture home and hang it on the wall and say, "This is what I mean." Instead, I take funny little symbols, make words, and paint with my imagination.

Writing will never recreate the truth of reality, but I can describe the substance of water, the feel of water on the skin, and the sound of water, and in doing so I bring a dream or a vision to the eyes and heart that recreates a memory or a desire for what the water can bring.

It is raining as I write. I like the rain, for all at once everything that we know is covered with water or with the sound of water, and we are for a moment a full community sharing a single moment, and we are not alone.

I wish I had the courage to abandon the umbrella in my life.

Part Two
COMPASSIONATE HEARTS

PERSISTENCE

Never, never, never give in!
—WINSTON S. CHURCHILL

It took Michelangelo four years of persistent labor to paint the ceiling of the Sistine Chapel in Rome. He did it standing on scaffolding and with the aid of assistants. His back hurt, he grumbled often that he was not a painter, he complained about his twisting spine and how much the paint splattered on his face, and yet he kept at it.

Perseverance is admirable, but there are hidden consequences. I felt such a consequence on my index finger a few days ago.

As I returned from a visit to the library, stepping out of my car in the driveway, I noticed to my right, along the small rock wall, a dark mass of flies. My first thought was of the impending winter, the sudden cold, and the flies must be gathering for a quick exit. As I approached, I realized that these flying acrobats were not flies but BEES! A swarm of persistent bees was swirling, buzzing, zipping back and forth in the air, and dipping into a large crack under one of the loose stones in the wall.

There are two ways for company to enter my house: through the front door, and through the side door beside the driveway. Most people walk along the driveway, beside the rock wall, and then they ring the doorbell. How could anyone possibly enter the house without being stung? That was the question which led me to the uncomfortable decision: I had to kill the bees.

Think of Michelangelo reaching up with his hand and brush illustrating God and all of creation on the ceiling of a church. The consequence of his labor is the beauty we can all see when we visit Rome.

Bees distribute pollen from flower to flower and suck up nectar. They carry the nectar back to the hive and after a mix of enzymes in their stomachs, after depositing the mixture into wax cells, it is transformed into honey. The consequence of their labors? Bees pollinate most of the crops we all depend upon for survival and produce a wonderful substance for breakfast.

However . . . although I can enjoy a piece of art on my ceiling, I cannot enjoy the consequences of a swarm of bees attacking the neighbors, the postman, or my family. So with a heavy heart (and a heavy can of Raid) I stepped out of the house, stood a good distance from the mouth of the crack under the rock, took aim as a gush of death shot into the dark space in the ground. Bees began to circle the entrance to the hive as they returned with their nectar. Bees stumbled out from under the rock. One bee attacked my index finger and stung me as I quickly brushed it aside and ran into the house.

The next morning, confident that they were gone, I opened the back door, walked down the steps to find fifty or sixty dead bees on the driveway, but hundreds more swarming, entering the dark wedge under the rock. I tried to cover the entire space with a large, plastic garbage bag hoping they would not be able to enter the hive and just go away. Instead, they found the edge of the plastic and simply flew under and made their way home.

I took the hose, set it on the jet spray and pumped a steady stream of water under the rock, but later in the day, they were back again, swarming, entering the hive, flying out from under the rock. I stepped into the garage, looking for anything I could throw at them: car wax, tire polish, turpentine, snow melt crystals. At this point, I felt as if they were using gas masks and hazmat suites to survive my attacks.

I did feel guilty. We need bees. But I also need a safe way to enter the house.

I decided to check the internet for advice. There were the typical suggestions about sprays and hiring exterminators, but there was also the idea that we ought to fill in the holes in our rock walls before the arrival of the bees. No one is going to fill the gaps in a rock wall on the chance a swarm of bees will make their way in, but it did make sense to me to plug up the hole to the hive, so I walked to the shed, picked up a shovel and my wheelbarrow. I filled the wheelbarrow with dirt, rolled the dirt to the rock wall and I began to shovel dirt into every crack and hole and under every loose stone that I could see. I packed the dirt, sprayed the entire wall with Raid, and the day was done.

This morning, I claimed victory as I stood on the driveway surveying the dead bees at the base of the dirt, seeing the air was free from the dark swarm.

Then two bees arrived.

They hovered over the place where the entrance of the hive once existed. I bet one bee turned to the other and said in bee language, "Huh?" Then they both, like retreating fighter pilots, zoomed upward, and disappeared over the forsythia bushes.

Whew!

Michelangelo belonged on the scaffolding with a brush in his hand. That was his place of work. This was mine.

AT THE TIP OF MY FINGER

Touch has a memory.

—JOHN KEATS

Many years ago, I read a book called *Dreams from My Father*. I liked it so much that I wrote a letter to the author, a young senator from Illinois, and sent him one of my books about my disabled brother. Soon enough I received a kind thank you, and a promise to read about my brother. He wished me luck and signed his name, "Barack Obama, United States Senator."

When President Obama was first elected, I opened a small wood box illustrated with zebras and elephants, shuffled through some papers, and found the letter. As I listened on the television to the president-elect give his victory speech in Chicago's Grant Park on November 4, 2008, I slowly ran the tip of my finger over his signature.

"To those—to those who would tear the world down," the president said, "we will defeat you. To those who seek peace and security: We support you. And to all those who have wondered if America's beacon still burns as bright: Tonight, we proved once more that the true strength of our nation comes not from the might of our arms or the scale of our wealth, but from the enduring power of our ideals: democracy, liberty, opportunity and unyielding hope." This man reminded us about hope and change.

As I touched the President's signature I said a little prayer for him, for his family, and for our country, as if I was rubbing a magic stone that would grant me a wish.

My wife, Roe, and I recently drove to Virginia because I always wanted to visit Mount Vernon, the home of George Washington. I was impressed with the house, and the gardens and the guide's explanation about Martha and how the President refused to be crowned king and refused to retain power after two terms as president. I was moved as I stood before Washington's simple, white sarcophagus. But what impressed me the most was the banister.

As we finished the first half of the tour of the famous mansion, we began walking up the stairs when the tour guide said that Washington wanted a new banister installed in the stairwell. I think the guide said it was made of oak, but I do remember him saying as I held onto the rail making my way up to the bedrooms that George Washington's hand once held the very same banister as he made his way upstairs. Touching the banister that George Washington touched was almost as great as when I touched Babe Ruth's bat at the Yogi Berra Museum in Montclair.

We make connections with people through the objects that we share. One of my favorite writers is Loren Eiseley, the Benjamin Franklin professor of anthropology at the University of Pennsylvania, who died in 1977. He was acclaimed as one of our nation's best literary stylists, writing about ancient tombs, our predicaments in the universe, the individual rediscovering himself or herself in the vivacity of humanism. And I remember, too, how he wrote about a broken clay pot.

Eiseley was at an archeological dig in the Middle East, I think, when he came upon a broken clay pot, and embedded in the small piece was a thumbprint. It was clear in the way he wrote that Eiseley was enthralled and moved that more than 2,000 years ago someone made a pot and inadvertently left behind an impression of his thumbprint. Eiseley placed his own thumb flat onto the potter's print.

We look for ways to reach beyond ourselves in search of answers or comfort.

One of my favorite philosophers is Martin Buber. In his best-known book, *I and Thou*, Buber wrote, "All real living is meeting." Human beings discover meaning in making connections in our relationships to others.

We hold the hands of those we love. We run our fingers over those things that we admire. As we touch the surface of our smartphones our fingers act as a conductor and close the gap between two separate conductive electrodes, similar to the way a light switch works.

When we close the gap of what separates us, we hear voices, we see light, we recognize who we are as a people, "one soul," as the poet Walt Whitman wrote.

We leave the world with a message: we need to grope in the darkness as if blind until we touch another human being who will lead us to unyielding hope and love.

SMART DAYS

If you want your children to be intelligent, read them fairy tales.
If you want them to be more intelligent, read them more fairy tales.
—ALBERT EINSTEIN

We are never as smart as we think we are. At different points of my life, I endured private, intellectual humiliations.

In third grade Sister Lillian was so angry with the class that she walked up to the front of the room, picked up a piece of chalk and with a loud bang smashed that chalk onto the blackboard and made a small dot.

"All your brains are as big as a pea, as big as this!" she growled as she ground the tip of the chalk into the board as if she was drilling into our heads how misbehaved we were. I do not remember what we did wrong, but I do remember how startled I was to learn that my brain was only the size of a pea.

I loved dinosaurs at the time and remembered my father saying that a stegosaurus had a brain the size of a lemon, so I really felt dumb when I found out that my brain was just as big as a pea. Made sense. A dinosaur, a creature much bigger than I was with a brain the size of a lemon, so of course my brain had to be smaller.

At the dinner table that night, when I announced to my family how worried I was that my brain was so small, my older brother nearly spit out a mouth full of mashed potatoes and my sister giggled.

In high school my science class visited a planetarium. After we all settled in our seats, the instructor welcomed us, and dimmed the lights as the great projector splashed the stars and universe above us on the domed ceiling.

"Here is Leo the Lion," the guide pointed as he projected a lion that connected the dots of the stars to form the shape of the lion.

"Here is Taurus the Bull," and again a bull was projected onto the ceiling and the stars fit the outline of the bull.

But each time the illustration of a constellation was removed, and we looked at the stars, no matter how hard I tried, I just could not see what the Greeks saw in the night sky. I didn't see a bull or a lion. The only constellation that I can clearly see is the Big Dipper. It really looks like a cooking utensil; I can see the outline clearly.

The poet Robert Frost called the stars "fireflies in the garden." I get that, the blinking stars like the flashing on and off of fireflies on a hot summer evening, but I always feel foolish when my brother-in-law points out, "There, Pegasus the Horse! There, Orion the Hunter and Gemini the Twins." I crane my neck, say ooh and ah and with a voice of authority say, "And there is the Big Dipper, the Cooking Pot." No one is impressed.

But there is one other intellectual misfire in my life that I rarely share with anyone. I didn't know until I was in my late twenties that the moon does not generate its own light. I must have been kissing a girl in the planetarium when that fact was shared.

There was logic to my thinking. There is sunlight and moon light, so of course the moon generates its own light, under its own power.

I probably, eventually, read about the moon in a magazine or newspaper. The moon is not a sun. The moon is a large chunk of debris that was cut from the earth after a huge Mars-size body collided with our planet billions of years ago and cut off what became the moon. The moon is inert, a dead satellite that does not crank out its own light.

When I was a kid my grandfather and I stood on the top of the Empire State Building in New York City, and he said that if I strain my eyes, I would be able to see England across the ocean. I squinted.

Perhaps we place way too much emphasis on education, knowledge, and degrees. Perhaps we need to place more whimsy into the minds of children. Whimsy and imagination are two of our lost values.

Let's tell them the moon has a giant candle in its belly. Let's tell the children that the stars are really the freckles of God. Let's tell them that their internal organs are made up of vegetables and spaghetti, and let's teach them how to squint.

COMPASSIONATE HEARTS

If you want to find Cherry-Tree Lane all you have to do
is ask the Policeman at the cross-roads.
—P. L. TRAVERS, *Mary Poppins*

Barney Fife, Andy's deputy sheriff in television's *The Andy Griffith Show*, was a kind but bumbling policeman who made sure everyone in Mayberry, North Carolina, followed the rules of law.

While some of our policemen and women today are brutes and lack wisdom and compassion, most are smart, caring human beings who truly serve their communities with dignity and courage.

"Your wallet just flew off the roof of your car!" That is not what my son Michael expected to hear from a man who zoomed up in his car to Michael's left, rolled down his window on a six-lane highway and shouted, "Your wallet!"

Michael was driving his cousin to Newark Airport. Before they left the house, he frantically looked for his wallet, could not find it and drove off just the same, for his cousin had to catch that plane. When the stranger called out as both he and my son were driving down the highway, Michael decided not to stop because he didn't want his cousin to miss his flight.

"When I drove home," Michael said, "I thought I had a pretty good idea where my wallet must have been, based on where that nice guy rolled down his window."

Michael pulled over to the side of the highway and began walking. "After a few minutes, I saw what I thought might be a wallet leaning against the concrete median in the middle of the highway, but I just wasn't sure, and then I looked down and there, a few inches from my left foot, was my Triple A card." It must be my wallet, Michael thought.

He watched the speeding cars rushing past him, "And then I timed it so that I could cross the highway." He made it to the median and, sure enough, there was his wallet, his empty wallet. "I was so disappointed. My driver's license, my Social Security card, my credit card." Michael said he was just about to start walking along the median in hopes of finding his things when a police car, with flashing light, pulled up in the fast lane, and a Wayne, New Jersey, police officer asked Michael what he was doing in the middle of the highway.

Michael said to me, "Dad, he was so nice. He told me to hop into the back of his car, and he drove me back across the highway to my car." "'I'll drive back on the highway and see if I can find your things,'" the policeman said, and the last thing Michael saw was the police officer driving slowly with his flashing red and blue lights up Route 23.

When Michael drove home, he was quickly on the phone with his bank. The bank placed him on hold, and then just as the bank representative returned and asked Michael for his credit card number, he received a call from the Wayne police. The officer had retrieved everything: Michael's license, his social security card, his credit card.

Say what you want about the world, how things are falling apart, that the news is bleak, the weather horrible, the state of the nation in economic decline. Ugliness is news because it does not happen all the time. Goodness is not news because it gushes all around us daily, minute by minute.

Henry David Thoreau in *Walden* wrote, "Goodness is the only investment that never fails." I would like to invest in the goodness of that stranger who zoomed down the highway after helping my son. I would like to invest in the goodness of the Wayne policeman who protected my boy.

We keep more in the wallets of our compassionate hearts than credit cards and driver's licenses.

THE WOUNDED SOUL

Upon this rock I will build my church.
—MATTHEW 16:18

Joe Scarborough, a former Republican congressman from Florida and host of the TV show "Morning Joe," quoted something that ought to rattle the national clergy, poets, dancers, artists, lovers, sea captains, Greek gods, Shakespeare, farmers, and anyone else who understands that under the veil of our physical existence resides a warmth of goodness, a power of humility, and an ethereal whisper that suggests a glory and passion that defines who we really are. Scarborough emphasized the Swedish philosopher Tage Lindbom's warning of the bleak harvest coming from a "secularized generation for which material existence is everything and spiritual life is nothing."

Cardinals in Rome walk around in their bright robes. Buddhists tell Rohingya Muslims in Burmese villages, "Leave or we will kill you all." Some Christians cherry-pick what works for their own ideologies. How did we all lose track of our ideals?

The material rules the day. Poets pander to contemporary fashions, creating work that has no music and no logic. Dancers on the New York stage are twisting and gyrating to the egos of choreographers. Artists tie an apple crate to a block of cheese and call it art. Lovers abandon love, sea captains race the clock, and Greek gods are ignored and lounging in a spa on Mount Olympus.

Shakespeare is being replaced with business management classes and Economics 101, and farmers infuse their soil and seeds with chemicals and genetic manipulations.

If we reject the spiritual aspect of all that we do, we become victims of time, money, comfort, isolation, and greed, and the flat surface of living rejects the topography of our souls.

The Catholic Church was built on a simple premise: love one another, not on laws that forbid divorced people to share in the meal of bread and wine with their community. I have to think the Church would be stronger, not weaker, if it were to remember in all things its first simple premise.

Buddhism is built on Dharma, meditation, the cultivation of loving-kindness and compassion, not on the intent of purification to eliminate neighbors who interpret God's existence in a different way. I'm referring again to those Buddhists in Burma, and the troubling news of what they have been doing.

A true poet writes from his vast reading experiences, has an innate ability, does not submit to his ego, collects words and images that flow like a symphony, and lovingly embraces beauty and wisdom in his gentle arms.

Art is built on an inborn talent mixed with countless years of practice. If we take any contemporary artwork in any modern museum and compare that work with Michelangelo's, we would be ashamed.

Love is built on patience and kindness, not lassoed around immediate gratification. Sea captains once dreamed of grand voyages, sea monsters, and adventure, not on the corporate schedule. Where is the adventure? Where is our wanderlust? The Greek gods gave us road maps to our strengths and flaws. Today's celebrities offer us air-brushed images and clichéd advice.

William Shakespeare wrote in *The Tempest*: "We are such stuff as dreams are made on, and our little life is rounded with a sleep." But now in college the world wants to fill the young not with dreams, but with ways to make more money. Is there a single student today who is praised by their parents for declaring a major in the humanities?

Ask a farmer today if he inhales the aroma of spring.

If we abandon the spiritual side of our living, if we pay homage only to the material world, we will, as Edna St. Vincent Millay wrote in her poem "The Pigeons,"

> *Walk in a cloud of wings intolerable,*
> *shutting out the sun as if it never had been.*

THE GIFT OF THE FIVE SENSES

By his very profession, a serious fiction writer is a vendor of the
sensuous particulars of life, a perceiver and handler of things.
His most valuable tools are his sense and his memory;
what happens in his mind is primarily pictures.
—WALLACE STEGNER, *On Teaching and Writing Fiction*

We were told carrots are good for our eyesight. We have been given the Statue of Liberty, Judy Garland's rainbow, the caress from those who love us.

A writer sells sensual memories, images outlined with aromas and colors that stream in his subconscious as if the lilacs were in bloom at his desk and his desk was cut from a box of crayons.

If we no longer live in paradise, our sensual bodies seem to refuse the banishment. Our five senses guide us back to nature and to what is truly important.

These are some things that I like to see, because, "After all, the true seeing is within" (George Eliot, *Middlemarch*):

-the abrupt point of an ice-cream cone
-the traceable border of an oak leaf
-the sensual letter S
-the exact square of a windowpane
-the gentle oval of an egg

-the powerful Great Pyramid of Giza
-young light green during the first days of spring
-the feathered white of an egret
-the smudged black of a bear
-the cool blue of an Italian ice
-cowered gray in a stone
-suggestive reds in a Japanese watercolor
-honey orange in the wings of the monarch butterfly
-fiery pink in a lotus
-dimpled raspberries.

And these are some of the sounds that I like to hear, because, "We two will pass through death and age lengthen / Before you hear that sound again with me" (Sara Teasdale, "I Thought of You"):

-sap crackling in a log fire
-brittle leaves crushed as we walk in autumn
-the spine of a new book breaking
-a gumball rolling down the chute of the gumball machine
-the wheels of a passenger jet touching the tarmac on landing
-the symphony of tree frogs and crickets during a summer night.

Some aromas I like, because, for instance, "At no other time [than autumn] does the earth let itself be inhaled in one smell, the ripe earth" (Rainer Maria Rilke, letter to Cézanne):

-the new crisp aroma of a new shower curtain

-musty delight in old books

-the romance of honeysuckle

-the nostalgia of baked bread

-eagerness for bacon

-the ease of inhaling the aroma of burning wood

-the satisfaction of cut grass

-the routine aroma of brewing coffee.

And these are just a few things that I like to touch because, as John Keats knows, "Touch has a memory":

-the tops of freshly cut bushes

-flowing water

-fine sand

-marshmallows

-a cold glass of soda

-a banister

-cats

-a shaved face.

Some things I like to taste because I agree with Thornton Wilder: "My advice to you is not to inquire why or whither, but just enjoy your ice cream while it's on your plate."

-chocolate ice-cream

-chocolate ice-cream

-chocolate ice-cream

-chocolate ice-cream

-ice-cream made from chocolate.

These are all gifts to us.

Do we know the difference between what our senses tell us and the reality of the world that surrounds us? In dreams we swoon at the fragrance of the rose, but in life the rose is a moment's decoration in the garden.

THE ACHE OF ALONE

Solitude is fine but you need someone to tell that solitude is fine.
—HONORÉ DE BALZAC

What is the difference between loneliness and solitude? This morning I think of the poem "Dance Russe" in which William Carlos Williams described the sun that is rising as "that flame white disk in silken mist above shining trees."

Williams, a doctor who lived all his life twenty-two miles from where I grew up, wrote in his poem, "I am lonely, lonely. / I was born to be lonely, / I am best so!" He knew that we may give birth to ourselves all over again in solitude, for in contemplation we see everything anew as a child sees a giraffe for the first time.

To live a life knowing the secret of things gives us freedom to sit like kings and queens among the riches of art, nature, and music without being sad.

Loneliness is the absence of love.

I think of the poor monster in *Frankenstein*, Mary Shelley's book. He was created out of the loneliness of Dr. Frankenstein, but the monster wandered throughout his short life trying to understand why he was not loved. "Shall I respect man when he condemns me? Let him live with me in the interchange of kindness, and instead of injury I would bestow every benefit upon him with tears of gratitude. . . . But that cannot be."

Just love me, the monster pleads, *and I will love you back*. He eventually realizes the reason for his loneliness: he is shunned and unloved. Because people pushed him away, he concluded, "If I cannot inspire love, I will cause fear." Loneliness eats away at our spiritual selves until we no longer know who we are.

I think also of poor Jay Gatsby in F. Scott Fitzgerald's famous novel. He was great because no matter the cruelty of the girl that he loved, he held onto his dream of winning back Daisy. He had no real friends. He was obsessed with Daisy and poured all his secret needs and secret self into the hope of earning salvation from a superficial woman who most of all enjoyed beautiful clothes, whose "voice was full of money." He created Venus in his imagination, a woman he would never find, a joy he would never attain, and this made him one of the loneliest characters in literature.

Rainer Maria Rilke wrote in one of my other favorite books, *Letters to a Young Poet*: "Love your solitude and try to sing out with the pain it causes you. For those who are near you are far away . . . and this shows that the space around you is beginning to grow vast . . . be happy about your growth, in which of course you can't take anyone with you, and be gentle with those who stay behind."

There is sorrow in solitude, for we have to learn to abandon the hope that others will satisfy our needs. We need to turn within ourselves and sing out our pain as Williams did in his poem. As we look within ourselves, we grow, we seek happiness in the space that surrounds us, and if we travel into the country of solitude fighting windmills, we will have a good chance to discover contentment.

In one of his most famous poems William Wordsworth says right away that "I wander lonely as a cloud." How well put, describing our individual lives "that floats on high o'er vales and hills." We all wander lonely in this world. Like Shelley's monster, Gatsby, and Williams . . . we all wander through our lives asking the same question: How do I satisfy my loneliness? Wordsworth in his sorrow happened upon "a host of golden daffodils / Beside the lake. . . ." He compared the flowers to the stars at night and he realized that a person cannot help but be happy in the presence of the beautiful flowers. He looked and looked at the daffodils and realized a wealth of wisdom can emerge from what nature brings. Wordsworth knew what it was like to sit on a couch when we are lonely and when to use our "inward eye" to see the "bliss of solitude" as we dance with the daffodils.

"Loneliness is the poverty of self," wrote May Sarton. Most of all, as she said, "solitude is richness of self."

SIGN IN PLEASE

I stopped believing in Santa Claus when I was six.
My mother took me to see him at a department store and
he asked me for my autograph.
—SHIRLEY TEMPLE

A few weeks ago, I visited a bookstore of used and antique books and found, for $12.50, *Sabbatical*, a hardcover novel by John Barth.

I became a huge fan of Barth's work after reading *Teacher*, a charming essay he wrote in 1986 in celebration of his wife, Shelly. She was a high school English teacher: bright, compassionate, and filled with a professional commitment that we all hope all teachers possess. John could not say enough about the qualities of his wife's skills:

At the front end of her forties, unlike some other high-energy schoolteachers, she has no interest in "moving up" or moving on to some other aspect of education. For her there is only the crucible of the classroom—those astonishing fifty-minute bursts for which, like a human satellite transmitter, she spent hours and hours preparing—and the long, patient, hugely therapeutic individual conferences with her students, and the hours and hours more of annotating their essays: word by word, sentence by sentence, idea by idea, value by value, with a professional attention that puts to shame any doctor's or lawyer's I've known. How I wish my children had had such a high-school teacher. How I wish I had had!

So, when I found a novel by Barth that I had not yet read, I was delighted. When I opened the book, I found that it was not only a first edition, but it was also one of only seven hundred and fifty copies that were specially bound . . . and it was *signed*.

I brought the book to the counter and said sheepishly to the proprietor, "Your book prices are extremely low." He was an old man with a wonderful smile. He said, "I like to see as many books as possible find new homes."

I love autographed books! John Barth spent five to six seconds writing his name in the book. His hands touched the pages, and now the book was in my hands. I felt a connection with the man. Once when I visited Robert Frost's house in Shaftsbury, Vermont, I felt a kinship with him as I looked out the living room window as he must have done many times in his life. I like that feeling.

I have the following autographed books: *To Kill a Mockingbird* by Harper Lee; *Conversations at Midnight* by Edna St. Vincent Millay; many books by Henri Nouwen and May Sarton. I have books signed by Kathleen Norris, Wendell Berry, Kenneth Rexroth. I have personal letters from President Reagan, President Obama, Eunice Kennedy

Shriver, and Fred Rogers. I have autographs of Arthur Miller and William Carlos Williams.

I am disappointed, however, when I see people sign their names with a pretentious, illegible flourish. I like thinking about some of the earliest autographs discovered on clay tables over five thousand years ago. I like going to art museums and seeing paintings with the signatures of Van Gogh, Monet, Pissarro, Dégas.

I remember my own frustration in first grade when I had to learn to write my name. Eleven letters! My name has eleven letters, and Sister Elizabeth Anne would not let me write just "Chris." No . . . I had to write "Christopher" on every work sheet, spelling test, and drawing exercise that we did in class . . . AND my last name! "Be proud of who you are," sister said. Eighteen letters to sign my way out of St. Luke's Grammar School and up to heaven.

Christopher deVinck

PENCIL WITH AN ERASER IS A SIGN OF HUMILITY

I think best with a pencil in my hand.

—ANNE MORROW LINDBERGH

March 30th is National Pencil Day. On this day in 1858 Hymen Lipman received the first patent for attaching an eraser to the end of a pencil.

When I first became a writer in 1974, I was a graduate student at Columbia University. I used a pencil. I sat in my graduate dorm room on 116th Street and scribbled my first poem on a sheet of white typing paper. I was lonely. The girl I loved refused my marriage proposal. I was trying to decide if I would join the Peace Corps, for I had just been accepted. With a pencil in hand, I tried to recreate the young woman, tried to shout in my room with the window open so that all of Manhattan could hear my scream of frustration and sorrow.

A pencil is a powerful tool. All you have to do is let the graphite tip touch paper and blood drains from the yellow shaft of the pencil, tears gush out, the ocean spreads out on the page. Touch a pencil point to a piece of paper and a woman appears with a bouquet of wildflowers in hand, or a boy turns into a lion in his dorm cage, pacing back and forth.

On January 12, 2018, Sam Anderson, a writer for the *New York Times*, began his delightful article about one of the last pencil factories in America with these words:

A pencil is a little wonder-wand: a stick of wood traces the tiniest motions of your hand as it moves across a surface. I am using one now, making weird little loops and slashes to write these words. As a tool, it is admirably sensitive. The lines it makes can be fat or thin, screams or whispers, blocks of concrete or blades of grass, all depending on changes of pressure so subtle that we would hardly notice them in any other context. (The difference in force between a bold line and nothing at all would hardly tip a domino.) And while a pencil is sophisticated enough to track every gradation of the human hand, it is also simple enough for a toddler to use.

Such good writing, and I like how he said that he was using a pencil at the moment he began writing this essay. And I agree. The pencil is a wonder-wand.

Henry David Thoreau not only worked in his father's pencil factory, but he also improved the quality of the pencil by mixing graphite with clay, and those pencils soon took over the market and were the pencils of choice. While his career took him to Walden Pond, we owe Henry thanks not only for adding to our American character through literature, but also for the improvement of the small stick of yellow wood.

The California Cedar Products Company, run by Charles Berolzheimer, is the world's leading independent supplier of wooden slats for the production of wood-cased pencils. On their webpage *pencil.com* they explain why most of our pencils are yellow:

During the 1800s, the best graphite in the world came from China. American pencil makers wanted a special way to tell people that their pencils contained Chinese graphite. In China, the color yellow is associated with royalty and respect. American Pencil manufacturers began painting their pencils bright yellow to communicate this "regal" feeling and association with China.

When I was a boy, I felt regal when I had a tall, yellow pencil in my hand. A pencil is 7.5 inches long. The average height of a boy at the age of eight is fifty inches. To a kid, that is a tall, important pencil. I also believed a story I heard that the architect who designed the Empire State Building was inspired by the shape of a pencil. Now that, I thought as a boy, was a pencil that deserved respect.

I like the smell of pencil shavings, and I never understood why we blow on the tip of a pencil after we pull it out of a sharpener. I do the daily crossword puzzle with a pencil because of my lack of confidence and the quick convenience of the eraser when I lose my way across and down. John Steinbeck wrote his books with a pencil. Yes, I admit I

Pencil with an Eraser Is a Sign of Humility   79

graduated from the pencil to the typewriter, and then to the magic of the computer and the word processor.

In 2012, Jim Leach, the former chairman of the National Endowment for the Humanities, interviewed another of our great writers, Wendell Berry, and asked: "You write by hand and, famously, do not own a computer. Is there some kind of physical pleasure to be taken in writing by hand?" Berry answered: "Yes, but I don't know how I'd prove it. I have a growing instinct to avoid mechanical distractions and screens because I want to be in the presence of this place. I like to write by the ambient daylight because I don't want to miss it. As I grow older, I grieve over every moment I'm gone from this place, because it is inexhaustibly interesting to me. Unexpected wonders happen, not on schedule, or when you expect or want them to happen, but if you keep hanging around, they do happen."

I don't know if Wendell uses a pencil or a pen, but that sense of being in a quiet place without the whirring distractions of lights, engines, and electricity, just being in the presence of a sheet of paper and a writing implement in the hand slows down the urgency to go, go, go and brings the mind and soul to really look at the words, and the self to feel the loops and slants of the letters and of our changing emotions.

Unexpected wonders happen . . . at the tip of a kiss, at the tip of a roller coaster, at the tip of Mount Everest, or at the simple tip of a sharpened No. 2 pencil.

THE LIGHT OF MY SONS

It's a father's duty to give his sons a fine chance.
—GEORGE ELIOT, *Middlemarch*

Today is Michael's birthday. He is my youngest son, who was born on March 31, 1985, in the morning.

March 31 is the ninetieth day of the year. On this date in 1889 the Eiffel Tower in Paris was officially opened. In 1918 Daylight Savings Time went into effect for the first time. Johann Sebastian Bach was born on this day in 1685. The poet Octavio Paz was born on March 31, 1914. And March 31 was also my father's birthday, nice bookends to my life.

The Eiffel Tower is 1,063 feet tall. Michael is 5'11" and a fireman in Jersey City, New Jersey. He climbs a 100-foot ladder that leans against a building that is gushing smoke and fire.

In the summers when the days were longer and the sunlight brighter, I remember watching Michael racing throughout the neighborhood on his bike with his friends. I watched him on the swing. I watched him rush into the house delighted that it was spring. Michael is one of daylight saving's gifts in my mind's eye.

Bach created the glorious *Brandenburg Concertos*. When I hear Michael whistling, I hear a symphony in my heart.

In Octavio Paz's poem "Piedra de Sol" (Sun Stone), he wrote, "To love is to undress our names." Michael is a Hebrew name meaning "Who is like God." When I think of God I think about mercy, kindness, generosity. . . Michael's personality traits.

In the Bible the angel Michael fought Satan and became the patron saint of soldiers. I am Michael's best soldier in his army.

Fathers want to protect their sons. When Michael was a boy and we took him to the arcade at the Jersey shore, I ached each time he didn't win a plush dog or a snake at the games. When I took him to Yankee Stadium and he brought his mitt, I ached that he didn't catch a fly ball. When Michael had surgery on his shoulder, when he tells me about a fire he helped extinguish, when I see the ugly side of the world in the news, I want to rush to Michael, grab him, and bring him home and protect him.

Atticus Finch in *To Kill a Mockingbird* felt the same about his son, Jem: "There's a lot of ugly things in this world, son. I wish I could keep 'em all away from you. That's never possible."

When I sit next to Michael I spontaneously smile. He is the type of person that lights up a room with his personality. When he beats me at chess (most of the time) I take delight in his clever moves.

Michael is a good son, a good husband to his wife, Lauren, a good brother to Karen and David, a good colleague at the firehouse.

On his son's first day of school, Abraham Lincoln wrote a letter to the boy's teacher. "It is all going to be strange and new to him for a while and I wish you would treat him gently," the letter began, and then the sixteenth president asked the teacher to take good care of the child.

Teach him that for every enemy, there is a friend.

10 cents earned is far better than a dollar found.

It is far more honorable to fail than to cheat.

Teach him to learn how to gracefully lose, and enjoy
*   winning when he does win.*

Teach him to avoid envy and the secret of quiet laughter.

Teach him to laugh when he is sad.

Teach him the wonders of books and to ponder the
*   extreme mystery of birds in the sky.*

Teach him to have faith in his own idea.

Try to teach my son the strength not to follow the crowd.

Let him have the courage to be impatient and the courage
*   to be brave.*

Teach him to have sublime faith in himself, because then he
*   will always have sublime faith in mankind, in God.*

These are the things that the father wished for his son. Lincoln ended the letter with these simple words: "See what you can do. He is such a nice little boy, and he is my son."

BOO!

I got a rock.
—CHARLIE BROWN

Halloween is meant to frighten us: ghouls, ghosts, and skeletons. My ninety-year-old grandmother resented the neighborhood decorations, reminders of the frail bones in her own hands, and of her own impending death.

Arthur Conan Doyle wrote in his Sherlock Holmes novel *A Study in Scarlet*, "Where there is no imagination, there is no horror."

We have heightened the meaning of Halloween, once considered the beginning of winter, the dark half of the year, or All Hallows Eve, the time to pray for recently dead members of the family. These days we think October 31 is all about mummies, gore, witches, and pranks.

But I think our culture has enough violence, death, and masked ugliness. A little charm and levity on Halloween aim to delight children and remind us that we all have a stake, not in Dracula's heart, but a claim to laughter and candy along the streets of our imaginations.

I was a hobo, the easiest costume to make: a bit of charcoal rubbed on my face, a seedy hat from the closet, a torn shirt. I was a cowboy in first grade, resenting the fake wool glued to my pants and a boy sitting next to me in class who called me a sissy. When I was a teenager, I thought it would be fun to dress up in my father's old tuxedo he used to go ballroom dancing in his youth and pretend that I was Charlie Chaplin. When I walked downstairs to exhibit my clever idea, my father looked up from the newspaper and said, sadly, "Take it off."

One Halloween my best friend Johnny and I realized we could cover more ground and ring more doorbells if we grabbed our bikes and zoomed around town to collect great amounts of Hershey Bars and Milky Ways, and those small paper bags people once gave out filled with candy corn and, if you were lucky, a quarter.

I decided one Halloween to re-create typical traditions for my own three children: bobbing for apples and running in the back yard with socks filled with flour. "Run in the yard and smack the trees and see the ghosts appear." They loved watching the flour bloom out of the socks and puff up into clouds of midnight phantoms.

If you want to create sure-fired entertainment for your children or grandchildren on Halloween, make tissue ghosts. Take two tissues, scrunch one in a ball. Take the other and drape it over the ball. Twist a bit of string at the base to make a head, place two, black magic marker dots for eyes, and let the children run with the ghosts trailing behind them on the strings.

Yes, of course, Halloween: moans from the grave, fake coffins on the lawns, William Shakespeare's brooding witches in *Macbeth*: "Double, double toil and trouble; fire burn, and cauldron bubble." I get it. Eye of a newt, bats, owl wings, a hell broth to cook on Halloween.

But I'd rather drink apple cider and entertain the mist of my own ghost that swirls around me whispering, "It is not time for death, but time to carve the pumpkin and answer the doorbell. The children are there."

THANKSGIVING

I wish the bald eagle had not been chosen as the representative of our country. The turkey is a much more respectable bird, and withal a true original native of America.

—BENJAMIN FRANKLIN

From a distance it looked like two dinosaurs emerged from the woods. I sat with my ninety-seven-year-old mother on the back porch of the house where I grew up as the creatures with long necks and wide bodies waddled out onto the open lawn.

"Here they come!" mother announced with delight. Out strutted the regal creatures, and the closer they came to the porch the more I realized they were two stout turkeys on a mission. "Start shelling the peanuts!" she said.

My father died seven years ago at 100. My mother keeps up with the news, writes daily, explains in vivid details the last novel she just finished reading. Yesterday she wanted me to pay particular attention to the burning bush planted in the front of the house forty-some years ago.

My mother looked at the turkeys and said, "They will eat the entire peanut, so I like to crack the shells open and just give them the inside to make it easier for them." She and I began shelling peanuts, and by the time I reach ten, the two turkeys were standing at attention at the bottom of the porch stairs.

"Last week they began climbing up the stairs. I didn't like that, so I shooed them away." Mother laughed as she tossed her shelled peanuts over the porch rail at the clawed feet of the turkeys. They immediately eyed and pecked quickly and gobbled up the small nuts with precision.

"Keep shelling, Christopher! Keep shelling!" she called out with glee. We continued to shell the peanuts vigorously, trying to keep up with the turkeys' expectations.

Mother shared with me how grateful she was when she and my father came to America in 1948 to start a new life after World War I and II ravished Belgium. "This house was perfect for us: the wood floors, the neighbors, the woods in the back." As she spoke, the sound of cracking peanuts underlined each of her words. "There were daffodils in the garden. Your father and I were startled with delight when we saw for the first time an exotic bird, a blue bird. We had never seen a blue bird in Belgium. It was a blue jay."

Then we laughed thinking how common a blue jay is and yet seeing a blue bird for the first time must have been wonderful. "And the red, red cardinals!" At dusk, having had their fill of peanuts, the turkeys started running down the lawn like taxiing 747s on the runway until they spread their wings and created enough lift to carry them up into the branch of the tall oak tree to roost for the night.

I like sitting with my mother on the porch as the sun sets. There is a honey glow on the trees and sky and on my mother's face. I am grateful to live in the United States. I am grateful for peanuts and for the burning bush and for the shimmers of the autumn light and blue jays. We all thirst, we are all in pain at times, we endure the husk of life, but often enough we are delighted with fat turkeys, wine, family, football, and our homes.

Most of all, I am grateful that I can still go home.

Part Three

THE WISDOM
OF HUMILITY

DREAMS OF SANTIAGO

You are never too old to set another goal or to dream a new dream.
—C. S. LEWIS

Many years ago, my family and I discovered the magical birch wood forest. You will not find it on any map. It did not have an international reputation as does the redwood forest of California.

If you drive slightly northwest from New York City for five hundred miles, you will come to Combermere, a small town in Ontario. Drive up Perrier Road and stop at my father's property. Walk past the little cabin to the right and follow the path straight on. You will pass my mother's favorite oak tree. Make a left past the old potato field. Walk around the beaver pond and up through the thick woods. Climb the small hill upward until you reach the first stone wall, and then walk some more until you come to the second stone wall. There, just on the other side, is where the fairy tale forest of young, lithe birch trees *once* stood as if waiting to rehearse a ballet.

When my sister and her family and my family came across this gentle green place where the sun illuminated the white spotted bark, where the entire scene looked like a painting from the brush of an artist, we all sat on the rock wall and admired the silence and beauty.

The birch forest doesn't exist any longer. As the trees grew, they edged each other out. The thicker they grew, the more difficult it was for the sun to nourish the leaves. The weaker trees died; the stronger ones flourished and dominated the soil. Today there are a number of large old birch trees leaning precariously in the weak light. No young trees. No magic. Gone.

In one of my favorite books, *The Unbearable Lightness of Being*, author Milan Kundera wrote, "Everything is illuminated by the aura of nostalgia." We walk through our lives adding images and experience to what we have already lived and when we do so, the memories change, our minds expand, we connect old knowledge with new knowledge, and we grow.

What we live today is illuminated by what we remember. The trouble begins for me when I try to pick up the pieces of my past and attempt to reconstruct the day, relive the feeling, glue back the torn pages of what I have already lived, and recapture the book of my life, wanting to reread and even rewrite the chapters.

That is not a good idea.

I had so much fun building my snowman the other day and each time I looked out the kitchen window, there he was with a huge smile on his face. For two days we experienced a January thaw. For a bit of time winter opened its frozen jaw and let us roam into a few days of warmth. Then one morning I woke up to see that not only did my snowman fall over, not only did most of the snow melt away, but also his face was scattered on the ground: two eyes, pipe and mouth, and nose.

I want to go sailing with my father again. I want to take my daughter to her first day of kindergarten again. I want to relive sledding with my brothers down the Lukaszewski's driveway and into the wide field below. Again. I want to go ice skating with my sisters down at the swamp and brush my mittens on the ice and see the goldfish swimming beneath us. I already want to rebuild my snowman.

In 1929 the hardware store in my little town of Pompton Plains, New Jersey, opened for the first time, and it has been run by the Jones family ever since. For the forty years that I have lived here, every December, Robbie, the grandson of the original Jones, sets up a two-dimensional wood cut-out of Santa, his sled and reindeer on the top of the store. The Christmas season began for me when I'd go to town for milk and see Jones's hardware store once again visited by St. Nick.

The other day, when I drove to town for milk, the Christmas display on top of the store was removed not only for the season, but forever. Robbie is retiring. His sons have taken different career paths. Home Depot and Lowe's have swallowed up the local hardware businesses, and Robbie is closing his store. It will be knocked down and a bank will take its place. A bank.

If I were Merlin or a god I'd lift the hardware store, carry it on my back and place it on a new foundation in the middle of a young birch forest growing somewhere in my past.

There is a beautiful statue in the Metropolitan Museum of Art in New York titled "Fragment of a Queen's Face." It isn't actually a full statue. It is just a broken portion, just the right side of her face and lips. It is more than 3,000 years old, Egyptian, made of yellow jasper, and beautiful. No one knows who the woman was. No one knows who the artist was. It is just a remnant, a broken artifact from the past that once represented someone whole. Standing before this piece makes me feel the sudden quiet of the museum, the silence of the woman, the slow drama of destruction: the face of the Egyptian woman, the face of my snowman, the smear of time blurring the memory of the birch wood forest.

Our memory is the album of the mind. Yes, we remember awful times. Yes, if we are bombarded with ugliness in our past, it is difficult to return to those pictures. But we also have memories of ice cream, a certain day on the beach, someone who loved us, the sound of my best friend, Johnny, calling out, "Come on, Chrissie! Let's ride our bikes to town and get some Superman comic books!"

Ernest Hemingway in *The Old Man and the Sea* had it right when he spoke about Santiago: "He no longer dreamed of storms, or of women, or of great occurrences, or of great fish, nor fights, nor contests of strength, nor of his wife. He only dreamed of places now and the lions on the beach."

As I look in the mirror at my own face, I sometimes feel the lost snowman with my own broken face.

I sometimes feel like Santiago, the old fishermen standing at the edge of the unforgiving sea no longer dreaming of storms or women or great occurrences. I only seem to dream about the birch forest and about the lion I felt I once was.

THE WISDOM OF HUMILITY

I wonder if the snow loves the trees and fields, that it kisses
them so gently? And then it covers them up snug, you
know, with a white quilt; and perhaps it says, "Go to sleep,
darlings, till the summer comes again."
—LEWIS CARROLL, *Through the Looking-Glass*

Captain! We can't hold onto the ship much longer! The storm is too powerful! We are being dragged under!"

"Abandon ship!"

"Aye, aye, Captain!"

This is how I felt last night while heavy snow kept piling up. I wanted to abandon ship.

No matter how much I shoveled, no matter how I maneuvered the snowplow, I couldn't keep up. During the day I shook the forsythia bushes again and again because they were being dragged to the ground. Thirty minutes after a good shaking and they were covered again, bent over, completely submissive.

I shoveled every thirty minutes. I freed the bushes every thirty minutes from 1:00 in the afternoon until the final struggle.

While I was in the driveway, in the dark by eight in the evening, I heard a crash down the street. A tree had fallen. That is when I realized that the heavy, wet snow was going to snap branches, and then I looked up and realized that my car sat under our maple tree out front.

I stepped into my car. The wind blew; the snow poured out of the sky in buckets. It was dark. The lights from the house illuminated the falling snow that looked like confetti. I drove the car five or six feet up the driveway, turned off the ignition, and stepped out just as a tremendous cracking sound exploded followed by a tremendous crash. A huge branch had broken from the maple tree, hitting the roof of the house, crashing through our dining room window.

Glass shattered in, too, onto the dining room table and into the kitchen. Part of the branch remained scattered on the driveway where the car had been just forty-five seconds before.

Because of the wind, the snow, and the broken window, because of the falling branches, and the driveway filling upon with more snow, because of the crippled bushes, I finally realized the battle was lost. I had to give up. The ship sank.

In Philip Roth's novel *Portnoy's Complaint*, he wrote, "It's a family joke that when I was a tiny child I turned from the window out of which I was watching a snowstorm, and hopefully asked, 'Momma, do we believe in winter?'"

I can assure Mr. Roth that I believe in winter.

The following morning, I called the insurance company, the power company, the tree removal company. I dug out the driveway, surveyed the damage, and vacuumed the glass shards from the dining room.

Then I had my breakfast. As I washed the spoon I had used for yogurt, and the knife I used to butter my toast, I looked out the window and saw a red cardinal peacefully pecking at the seeds in the birdfeeder.

WHO ARE YOU?

We have to dare to be ourselves, however frightening or strange
that self may prove to be.
—MAY SARTON

Sorrow is in my own back yard, hidden at the moment under a
foot of snow from the recent storm. The snow is like a mask
hiding the true identities of the lilac bushes and the boxwoods. The
humble pine trees look like tall kings and queens dressed in ermine
fur, and the grass looks like an ivory-coated Sahara Desert.

What masks do we wear? The restrictions of our clothes. Our
guarded facial expressions. Desires tucked away inside the shroud of
a winter shawl that conforms to the contours of our aching bodies.

I liked my self-confidence when I was young like the magnolia
blossoms in spring. As a teenager I was a lifeguard with the body of
a lifeguard: broad chest, firm legs, dark brown hair. I was confident
and filled with ego while standing in my bathing suit with a whistle
dangling from my neck. If it had been appropriate, I would have been
comfortable being myself like Michelangelo's statue of David that
stands nude and powerful in the Accademia Gallery in Florence, Italy.
But the skin of youth, like the melting snow out my window, reveals
the wrinkles of the old earth, the crevasses of age, the bones of the
bare maple tree that is my body.

In 2013, a preserved, fully grown 39,000-year-old wooly mammoth was discovered trapped in glacial ice in Siberia. Its hair was matted, its body covered with bald patches. Even blood was recovered with the possibility of cloning the creature into existence. This is how I feel today: balding with matted hair, and a desire to be cloned into youth. Why is it that our happy memories are frozen in the glacial ice of our minds? I can recreate those memories, but only from afar, only with dissecting tools as a scientist, not as a wild cowboy riding on the back of the powerful wooly mammoth.

Under the snow is the spot where my children's sandbox sat. Under the snow is where the swing set rocked back and forth. Under the snow is the place where the children danced in and out of the sprinkler and caught fireflies in the summer nights.

Shed the mask and we discover who we really are inside. Am I like Jonah flailing inside the belly of the whale, locked in, fearful of being digested for the creature's lunch? The monster of age eats away at us slowly. My hearing is already impaired. My muscles ache with the slightest exertions.

After a snowfall I like to see if I can find deer tracks. When I was a boy, I thought I could follow the tracks and see where the deer live. Maybe I could find my own way to C. S. Lewis's Narnia and watch the deer dance around a fire, or coat themselves with snow and branches from the holly trees as they prance, buck, and stomp the landscape with their hooves and grace.

The newspaper is still delivered to my house. It is tossed from a car window and lands on the front lawn. Each morning I step outside, happy to find the paper conveniently waiting for me.

Yesterday's paper and the world's woes were buried under the snow. I didn't know where it was. It is still there, perhaps nature's way of reminding us that the force of snow and winds is far more powerful than our ephemeral lives, but then the snow will melt and the world will once again be revealed: shootings, nuclear warheads, drugs, hunger, and genocide.

"Who are you?" the caterpillar asked Alice in Wonderland as he sat on his mushroom.

I hope that when the sun melts away the winter of who I am will find the rich loam of myself again prepared to blossom, prepared to push my daughter again in the swing, prepared to push the woolly mammoth across the ice and join the deer in some faraway land, the land of the past, the land of youth, the land hidden under the snow, a final resting place where I am not yet prepared to go, a wonderland with lots of comfortable mushrooms.

THE TREASURES WITHIN US

A good heart is worth gold.
—WILLIAM SHAKESPEARE, *Henry IV*

Many families carry with them, from generation to generation, myths and legends about a distant relative, or a crazy uncle, or a vague memory about a grandfather who fought in World War I. When I was a boy, my father, my uncles, and aunts reminded me over the years that we were all directly related to the painter Peter Paul Rubens.

I like Dylan Thomas's poem "A Child's Christmas in Wales" where he recalls the legend of a dotty aunt who, after a fire in the house, walked downstairs, looked at the chaos of smoke, firemen, and hoses, and said with conviction, "Does anyone want something to read?"

We pass along these stories to our children and grandchildren because some are funny, some tragic, but all carry an emotional spark that reminds us how we are connected. Loren Eiseley, the anthropologist from the University of Pennsylvania, wrote about the awe he felt while excavating a site and discovering a 2,000-year-old broken pot with the thumb print of the potter imbedded in the clay. How connected Eiseley felt over the hundreds of years to the ancient artist.

This past Christmas I was sitting beside my mother, and she was reminiscing about the Christmas days of long ago, how instead of electric light bulbs people used real lit candles in their Christmas trees, and kept buckets of water to the side as insurance that the tree, the house, and all of Belgium would not burn to ashes.

She spoke about the extraordinary treat of receiving that rarest of rare fruit in her stocking: an orange. Then she paused and said, "Your grandmother was the most generous person I ever met."

My grandmother sent me shoes from Belgium for my birthday. When she arrived for a summer visit, she brought Belgian chocolates, gummy mice (long before anyone in this country knew about gummy bears or gummy anything). She brought delicious marzipan pears and strawberries and the famous cookies from the city of Dinant. One summer she pulled out of her enormous suitcase a cuckoo clock for me! A cuckoo clock!

My mother leaned back in her chair and smiled and said, "Your grandmother once read about the possibility that doctors could perform eye transplants."

My brother Oliver was blind at birth.

My mother looked into my eyes. "Your grandmother said, 'I have lived a long life.' At sixty, she offered to give her eyes to Oliver. She said that she had her eyes for so many years and that she could now live without them and would gladly give Oliver her eyes so that he could take a turn and see."

Perhaps I have a bit of DNA from Peter Paul Rubens. Perhaps the ghosts of the Belgian aristocrats bump into me as they adjust their ascots and pipes, but they are not the true heroes in the history book of my life.

I think about my grandmother who survived the horrors of World War I and World War II. I think of this old woman who looked a bit like Mrs. Tiggy-Winkle in Beatrix Potter's story: stooped, unassuming, industrious. At the end of the story, Lucie retrieved her three handkerchiefs that the washer woman meticulously cleaned and ironed, and then as Mrs. Tiggy-Winkle ran back up the hill, Lucie suddenly realized "Why! Mrs. Tiggy-Winkle is nothing but a hedgehog!"

My grandmother believed that doctors could actually transplant her eyes and give them to Oliver. Anyone looking at my grandmother would simply exclaim, "Why, she is nothing but an old woman!"

In my eyes, my grandmother on that Christmas day was Joan of Arc, Mother Teresa, Rosa Parks, Helen of Troy, Antigone. She offered her eyes so that my brother might see. I will tell my grandchildren about my grandmother's offer. We live with the wild fiction of the past and with the gold world of enduring truth.

REAL MEN

I'm strong to the finish 'cause I eats me spinach.
—POPEYE THE SAILOR MAN

ast night three large trucks with yellow flashing lights were suddenly parked in front of the house. After a heavy snowstorm, trees fell and power lines were severed all over the state. Because the governor invoked a state of emergency, and because so many people lost electricity, power companies from different parts of the country arrived to help in the recovery.

The crew last night was from Georgia, over 800 miles away, and yet there they were, stepping out of the trucks with flashlights on the tops of their hardhats, men in heavy work pants and bulging tan coats with bright orange reflecting material. They all had beards, spoke with charming Southern accents, and looked like they could easily have been Robin Hood's gruff merry men of Sherwood Forest.

There are many stereotypes that represent different types of men: weak, strong, thin, large, leaders, followers, wise guys, peacemakers, lovers, haters.

My hands are soft. I never held a tool long enough to develop calluses. My skin is pale, having never been out on the farm or on a construction crew earning a deep tan. I never poured molten steel at the steel mills, climbed a fireman's ladder, boxed like Hemingway, conquered the west like John Wayne, capped a gushing oil rig, or drove a truck. I write poetry, for God's sake.

When I visited the New York City tomb of Ulysses S. Grant, that great Civil War general and President of the United States, I thought about the hundreds of thousands of men who died for what they believed, burly brave men with rifles, beards, and tattered uniforms. Gruff, rough Grant and the gruff, rough men of war.

One of the crew members from Georgia spat. I thought of Popeye chewing his spinach that gave him muscles and courage. The tall men who towered over me last night must eat lots of spinach. When I said to the crew that I had just the week before driven through Georgia, one who looked like Tom Selleck with his well-trimmed mustache and smile of authority asked, "Do you know the temperature in Georgia? We've been here in the snow for almost a week. I sure could use some Georgia sunshine."

My father said to me many times, "Christopher, you have four hundred years of gentlemen in your background." It is true that I am a Belgian baron, descendant of the painter Peter Paul Rubens, son of an author and college professor. I never slept in a tent, climbed a mountain, drank at a bar, rode a motorcycle, owned a gun, grew a beard, or played sports.

Standing on my toes and pushing out my chest a bit, I asked the fellow who was obviously in charge, "How do my wires look?"

"Your power line is nearly detached from your house. Easy to fix. We'll be gone in no time."

He may have well said, "That power line is like the jaws of a flame throwing dragon. No problem, I'll grab its tail and stuff it in my pocket in no time."

These were men's men. They would have made a good team on a pirate ship or on a mission as marines.

Most street power lines have 7,200 volts. The transformer reduces that down to 240 volts for our homes. To me that means 240 electric poisonous snakes are ready to bite me all at once.

"Easy to fix. We'll be gone in no time," said the man with a flashlight attached to his hardhat. Now, that is a man, a manly man.

Of course, I do not know these men from Georgia. All I saw was their professional strength and experience. I did not meet their wives or hear about their children or their dreams. I do not know about their happy memories or their soft sides. True men lasso wild horses and ride to visit their sweethearts.

I like so much the autobiography of President Grant. Think of his fame, his career as a general in war, his tough resolve to save the Union. Think of the famous Civil War photograph of Grant leaning against a tree, and then read his words about his other life, his soft self, attached to the burly side of what it means to be a man:

From that age until seventeen I did all the work done with
horses such as breaking up the land, furrowing, ploughing
corn and potatoes, bringing in the crops when harvested,

hauling all the wood, besides tending two or three horses, a cow or two, and sawing wood for stoves, etc., while still attending school. For this I was compensated by the fact that there was never any scolding or punishing by my parents; no objection to rational enjoyments, such as fishing, going to the creek a mile away to swim in summer, taking a horse and visiting my grandparents in the adjoining county, fifteen miles off, skating on the ice in winter, or taking a horse and sleigh when there was snow on the ground.

Some men wear uniforms, chew tobacco, lift weights, plough, haul in wood, but they also swim in the creek, visit their grandmothers, skate on the ice in winter, and take a sleigh ride.

This morning there are many boot prints in the snow in my front yard, evidence that men were here last night.

EMBRACE PASSION

To be sensual, I think, is to respect and rejoice in the force of
life, of life itself, and to be present in all that one does, from
the effort of loving to the making of bread.
—JAMES BALDWIN

Snow again. I am sitting on the cranberry couch reading a
biography of Colette by Judith Thurman. Stuart is curled up at
my side as cats do. Looking out the window I feel as if I am living in
Siberia.

As I read the book about the French writer I feel as if I am living
in the late 1800s during a time when women were repressed,
compressed, and distressed.

Colette's mother said, "You're not like me. I resist my passions,"
and warned her daughter that human touch might wilt Colette's
intact beauty. The young woman would have nothing of this. She
stepped out of the accepted expectations for women and forged
her life as an independent thinker, lover, and writer. She lived her
passions, pursued euphoria, succumbed to the caresses of pleasure,
and wrote her way to her own inner peace.

Stuart just rolled on his back and looked up at me as if asking,
"Please rub my stomach."

Cats are sensual. Pet me. Caress me. Hold me. They knead us with
their paws, purr in our presence, sleep on our laps, and desire warmth.

We human beings are sensual. When it snows, I like to stand outside on the deck for a moment, tip my head back and feel the individual cold flakes melting on my warm face. In the spring I like to hold a newly unfurled maple leaf and gently rub it against my cheek. I like the jolt of cold water against my body when I run into the Canadian lake during our summer vacation as I float on my back and feel the Canadian sun caress my face and chest.

We could all use a bit more sensuality in our lives. Our hands are meant to caress the back of someone we love, to massage the hair, to stroke a shoulder. Our skin is built to feel pleasure, our eyes to admire beauty, our voices to express affection. We all seek love overtly, and if love does not come to us, we seek love covertly, in our dreams, in a book, in the opera, or snowstorm.

We can learn from cats. A cat harrumphs onto our beds with honesty. "I want to sleep against your body." A cat rubs against our legs. "I am hungry. Feed me." A cat follows us no matter where we are in the house. "I like being with you."

Colette famously wrote that "time spent with a cat is never wasted." Time spent with those we love is never wasted.

We sometimes confuse our sensual pleasure with euphoria. Mmmmmm. Ice cream. That is close to euphoria, but it is only ice cream, an ephemeral pleasure. The visual euphoria of a late winter storm: the plump snow on the bushes, the snow lace floating down from the sky . . . but then the work with a snow shovel and the mess.

I believe there is no such thing as permanent delight. We feel hints of euphoria at a dance, at the creation of a poem, or at the revelations we experience during a beautiful sunset, but if we give up our pursuit of euphoria, we may as well die.

In her speech on being elected to the Belgian Academy, Colette said, "You must not pity me because my sixtieth year finds me still astonished. To be astonished is one of the surest ways of not growing old too quickly."

I take a lesson from Stuart and curl up on the couch and purr. I look at the snow with astonishment and continue reading my book.

HOLY SOUNDS

Within the sound of silence
In restless dreams I walked alone . . .
—PAUL SIMON

This morning in the stillness I heard a drip, drip, drip. The yard was under a foot of snow. The stone table on the deck looked like a giant mushroom. The sun was hidden behind lingering clouds. I heard in the distance a neighbor pushing a snow shovel. There were no cars running. No birds. But there was this constant dripping noise, an annoying drip, drip, drip.

Many years ago, I bought an antique regulator clock. It is made of oak; it has a pendulum and I have to wind it once a week with a large key. For years, in the evening I stopped the clock at 10:00 so that I would not hear the ticking when I was in bed for the night. Even though the clock was downstairs in the living room, even if I closed my bedroom door, I could still hear tick, tick, tick, tick . . . and couldn't sleep. Each morning after I showered and dressed, I'd walk downstairs, reset the clock, push the pendulum and the clock would regain its purpose.

Many people suffer from acute misophonia, a hatred of sound. I do not hate sound. I listen to the *Planets* by Holst, the choral music of Morten Lauridsen and Ola Gjeilo. I like very much the work of Dan Forrest, Stephen Paulus, Ēriks Ešenvalds. I like hearing the passenger jets flying in the distance, the sound of the chimes of the town clock announcing the hour. But dripping water at night, or the sound of a clock's gears, keeps me awake as I wait for the next drip or the next tick.

I do not hear the cry of hunger from across the ocean. I do not hear a child who is thirsty weeping in the land of deserts. I listen to the *Requiem* of Mozart, but I do not hear the suffering of those who are dying, or those who endure the loss of a father or brother to war, plagues, exterminations, murder, greed, anger. Drip. Drip. How do I edit the sounds of life from what it is that I want to hear and what I want to ignore? There is a cacophony of sorrow. Drip. Drip. There are cries in the shadows. Drip. Drip. Loneliness owns its own sounds: a whispered hello, a muted plea for love, a song sung in an empty house. Drip. Drip.

Where is your holy place? Where are you when you are alone, and you hear the tug of silence? In bed? At church? Walking under the elms in spring? Walking along the summer beach with your sandals in your hand? What is it that you think about in the silence? Love? Children? A nearly forgotten embrace? The voice of your mother? We covet silence and yet sound is one of the keys to our emotions, unlocking memories or voices that speak our names. Drip. Drip. But a sound that bangs like the blacksmith at his anvil distracts me, erases moments of contemplation and makes me anxious.

I stood up trying to figure out where the dripping sound was coming from. There was no leak in the roof of this little room. The kitchen faucet was closed.

What was that sound, that hideous sound? It was like a drumbeat against my senses. Drip. Drip. What horror? What misery? This dripping sound really wasn't the breath of a monster, but I was reminded of Edgar Allan Poe's story "The Tell-Tale Heart."

If you remember the story, the narrator murders old man and hides the body under the floorboard. The murderer believes he hears the dead man's heartbeat. "It was a low, dull, quick sound – much such a sound as a watch makes when enveloped in cotton." Yes, the low, dull, quick sound. The murderer heard his own guilt, or perhaps his own heartbeat.

I realized the dripping sound was coming from outside. I walked to the door that leads to the deck, and there it was . . . coming from the roof. While it had snowed vigorously the night before, the morning sun was already melting the snow, and the water was beginning to drip from the roof and onto the small metal grill that I leave out all winter.

The tick of our human heart can be heard with a stethoscope; the pulse of humanity can be heard in the novels and poems that we read, or in the cries and whispers we hear in the universal plea for mercy.

In the drip, drip, drip, drip of our lives we can see beauty in the hard paint swirling in the images that hang in the museums. We can measure the rhythmic sounds we hear during a swoon in the arms of a lover.

I moved the grill and I no longer hear the constant dripping sound. Drip. Drip. Tick. Tick. Time is running out.

INVENTION

Where there is no hope, it is incumbent on us to invent it.

—ALBERT CAMUS

We often notice when something is just right—the coffee temperature, the position of a chair, a relationship—and then we act: sipping the hot coffee with the satisfaction of the warm cup in our hands, sitting with a book in the chair at just the right angle with the lamp, or that feeling for someone else that lets us know a new friendship is developing.

This morning, after the newest snowfall, I stepped outside to fill the bird feeder when I noticed the snow was wet and heavy, just right to build a snowman, my new friend.

I felt a bit like Ebenezer Scrooge at the point of his conversion when he was filled with childlike glee.

"I don't know what to do!" cried Scrooge, laughing and crying in the same breath; and making a perfect Laocoön of himself with his stockings. "I am as light as a feather, I am as happy as an angel; I am as merry as a school-boy. I am as giddy as a drunken man."

Snow! I do know what to do! It is just the right snow! I am not sixty-six years old! Look at the beard of snow on the bushes! Look at the snow outlining the houses in the neighborhood, the trees, and the very existence of what surrounds us! It is as though winter underlined all that we see to emphasize the beauty! I am as merry as a schoolboy! I will build a snowman!

The last snowman I built was with my three children over thirty years ago. But I never forgot how: wait for the right kind of snow . . . heavy and wet; roll three large balls and stack one on top of the other. Use a carrot for a nose, stones for eyes and buttons, sticks for arms, and small pebbles to make a mouth that smiles.

The Danish writer Hans Christian Anderson wrote a fairy tale in which a new snowman didn't know what the strange but beautiful orbs were in the day and night. A wise old dog explained that those things were the sun and moon. "What you see yonder is the moon, and the one before it was the sun."

Then the naive snowman saw a young man and a young woman enter the garden. They were laughing and smiling.

"But what are they?" asked the snowman.

"They are lovers," said the dog, and then the dog spoke about the warm house and a beautiful stove. The snowman was intrigued by the idea of love and when he saw the stove for the first time he too fell in love.

The dog warned that the snowman should not go near the stove.

"You must never go in there," said the dog, "for if you approach the stove, you'll melt away, away."

But the snowman knew time is short, life is fleeting. "I might as well go," said the snowman, "for I think I am breaking up as it is."

The wise dog lamented that love was a terrible disease.

Of course, the snowman could not pursue the stove, and then he melted as the sun increased its power day by day, and where the snowman once stood there remained the stove's shovel. The boys who built the snowman had used the shovel as the inside support of the snowman's inner structure.

Part of the stove was deeply embedded inside the core of the snowman. Who we love becomes a part of who we are even as we slowly melt away. Love survives.

The snowman in the fairy tale kept asking questions, kept seeking a truth beneath the surface of his existence.

When I finished my snowman, I gave him a red scarf and a hat to keep him warm, and then I went inside for supper.

Later in the evening after reading, when it was time for bed, I placed my book on the coffee table and turned off the living room lamp, and when I looked out the window I felt a strange, lonely feeling, for there in the late glow of the streetlight I saw my snowman standing in the middle of the yard still smiling. It is absurd to feel empathy for a snowman. But I am reminded of the Greek myth about the sculptor Pygmalion who fell in love with one of his statues and the statue came alive.

In George Bernard Shaw's play, based on the myth, which later became the stage musical and film *My Fair Lady*, Higgins says to the common flower girl: "The great secret, Eliza, is not having bad manners or good manners or any other particular sort of manners, but having the same manner for all human souls: in short, behaving as if we were in Heaven, where there are no third-class carriages, and one soul is as good as another."

Of course, the snowman in my yard has no soul. He was made of crystal water and my effort. But for a few days he will be the center of the yard, a sentry smiling day and night under the sun and moon, and we know that he will, like us, soon melt into the ground and disappear.

Maybe the yard is heaven.

HUNGER

There are people in the world so hungry, that God cannot
appear to them except in the form of bread.
—MAHATMA GANDHI

In the film *Field of Dreams*, we hear again and again the famous
whisper, "If you build it, he will come." Ray Kinsella, played by Kevin
Costner, heard a voice that guided him throughout the film to conjure
up his father's spirit. Build a field of dreams and your father will return
to you. Unfortunately, that famous phrase morphed into, "If you build
it, *they* will come." If you build a casino, a resort, a luxury apartment, a
movie complex, people will come and spend their money.

I watched a special on television last night about a billionaire who
commissioned the building of his exotic summer mansion. Once it
was complete, the anxious team waited for the new owner's first walk-
through approval. The man was delighted with the marble floors and
the gold forks and knives on the table. He was impressed with the
lavish leather furniture. The chandelier looked like the fire of the gods
from Mount Olympus. "Yes," the wealthy man said. "This gives me
the right flavor for a summer getaway."

I think about our small cabin in Ontario, Canada, as my family
huddles around a kitchen table in the summer and we have pork and
beans on paper plates and we use plastic forks and paper cups, and
we are delighted.

While I abhor the unequal distribution of wealth in the world, while I look at that billionaire and think of the mud huts people consider home, when I think of the wealthy man's marble floors and the dirt floors of many schools in the poorest countries in the world, I feel hypocritical myself.

We own a second home in Canada. It has a blue roof, three floors, a stove, electric heat, and a bathroom with hot, running water. This house sits abandoned ninety percent of the time during the year. So, who is deaf to the poverty of the world? The man with his gold-plated forks, or the man with paper plates who will spend two weeks on his own little beach at the lake reading the poetry of Wallace Stevens while sipping a glass of lemonade?

Of course, I believe in working for what we have. Any sort of wealth does not just appear in the backyard. Farmers plant. Investors take risks. Bakers bake. I also do not think there is anything inherently wrong with people who want more: land, money, or luxury, but not at the expense of others. There is a difference between greed and success.

I think of industrious honeybees. They seek out a hole in a tree or a crevice in the rocks, and once they find their home, they chew wax until it becomes soft. From that extraordinary labor they build little cells into a honeycomb, a place to store their honey, to tend to the queen bee, to survive in their colony.

It is February. What do we learn from honeybees in winter? How do they survive the cold? Their labor begins with the flowers and the collection of nectar taken in the mouth and ingested. To survive we need to also come up with an idea and collect the needed tools, and we need to work.

The bodies of the bees transform the nectar into honey. Bees are born with this mechanism, as we are born with an intellect to manage our own transformations.

The more honey the bees store, the better their chances of survival in winter. The more we transform our energy and labor into useful goods, the better we can survive in our own lives.

When it gets to be below 57 degrees Fahrenheit, the bees form a circle around the queen with their heads pointing toward her. They feed on the honey, and when it gets even colder, the bees form a tighter circle and vibrate their wings to produce heat. Bees vibrating in their hives in winter produce enough heat to raise the temperature to 93 degrees.

If there are people without shelter, we ought to build, and they will come. When the world is hungry, we ought not to feed the world with gold forks. When the world shivers from the cold, we ought to all form a circle and close in together tighter and tighter to create heat for everyone.

Both Mahatma Gandhi and the Rev. Frank Bachman, an evangelist from the 1930s, are credited with these words: "Earth provides enough for every man's need, but not every man's greed."

KEEPING TIME

Yesterday is gone. Tomorrow has not yet come.
We have only today. Let us begin.
—MOTHER TERESA

A t the stroke of noon each day my wife and I walk through our little town of Pompton Plains, New Jersey. You can get a good ice-cream cone over at Curly's, and people are happy to know that the famous former Yankee ball player Derek Jeter was born right here in the small hospital. But this morning, as the cold chill of winter begins to blow in from the north, something seems amiss.

Our municipal building, constructed in the appealing colonial style, has a clock tower, and for the past month the clock has read 2:20. No matter what time of day, it is stuck at 2:20. We are expected to believe in our governments large and small, and when I see the clock that sits on top of the offices of our mayor, our police station, and our tax assessor, it makes me wonder what other small things are being neglected in those offices.

And then there is the timing of the Christmas season. There isn't anyone saying, "On your mark, get set, go to the mall and the internet. It is now the Christmas season." But in our little town, Robbie Jones at the hardware store each November used to set up Santa Claus and his reindeer in a charming, old-world display on the roof of his store. Norman Rockwell couldn't have imagined a better scene, and every November it signaled to the town that Christmas was right around the corner. But as my wife and I walk through town, we lament that the store is gone, replaced by a bank, and the little timepiece on the roof of the hardware store is also gone.

I like knowing that the town works like a clock: reliable, responsible, and even whimsical, so it disappoints me seeing that the weathervane on the top of the library is bent over, a useless mechanism, always indicating that the wind is not only coming from the south but also heading down the roof and into the parking lot.

Milan Kundera wrote in one of my favorite novels, *The Unbearable Lightness of Being*, "Human time does not turn in a circle; it runs ahead in a straight line. That is why man cannot be happy: happiness is the longing for repetition."

I liked the repetition of the train passing in the distance at the same time each day. But the train is gone. I liked measuring the time of day with the children returning from school, but they are all grown and living in their own time zones.

On December 15, 2021, my mother, at the age of 99, died peacefully in her sleep. Two months later my granddaughter was born. Kundera is right. Time runs in a straight line, but if we carefully pay attention, we can hear the ticking of our own hearts, trace the time of day based on the position of the sun, and at this very moment it is noon and I hear the bells from the Dutch Reformed church striking twelve times and I call out to my wife, "Are you ready for our walk?"

Part Four

WHERE IS LONG AGO?

WHERE IS LONG AGO?

Boy, why are you crying?
—J. M. BARRIE, *Peter Pan*

This morning cloudy, forty-three degrees, precipitation nil, humidity sixty-one percent, wind from the southwest at four miles per hour. Easter.

I realize as a Baby Boomer I am getting old, but I still want to go back, back when my daughter Karen reached out asking me to pick her up, back when Michael ran out to the yard with extended arms, "The crocuses are out! The crocuses!", back to the days when I took David to the airport and we watched the planes soar over our heads and we shouted together and waved our hands hoping the pilots would wiggle the wings of their planes. I want to go back and color Easter eggs with my children all over again.

I understand the cycles of life. The earth rotates around the sun clicking off each day like a giant clock. Each month is torn from the calendar one at a time with a single swipe of our hands. "I suppose it's like the ticking crocodile, isn't it?" J. M. Barrie wrote in his famous book *Peter Pan*. "Time is chasing after all of us."

I remember helping my ninety-year-old grandmother in bed as she sighed, "Life is so short, so short, Christopher." I'd kiss her forehead and she'd smile, a smile of eternity.

I am a bit sad this morning. No eggs to color.

All my children were born in Pompton Plains, New Jersey. We loved this town: the parades, the fireworks, and the lake in the summer; sledding, snowmen on the front lawn, Christmas in the winter. Our children were in Little League and Cub Scouts. Roe and I, we were a little family, taking the children to the famous ocean lighthouse in Sandy Hook pretending we were in the movie *Pete's Dragon*. We rode the little train in the county park; we laughed at the monkeys in the local zoo.

"Take me back, Clarence," George Bailey begged the angel in the film *It's a Wonderful life.* "Take me back."

I watched my children graduate from high school and college.

Each night, before I go to bed, I look inside the three rooms of my children . . . David, Karen, and Michael. They are all dear to me, their small voices, the forgotten shadows, the stories I told at their bedsides, the dog they loved, the cat that sat beside them as they played Monopoly.

I want them back.

I know. I know this is not the way the world works. Karen is happily married to Brian and living in Portland, Oregon. David the doctor and Emily the fiber artist are happily married. Michael is a firefighter in one of the largest cities in New Jersey and is married to lovely, smart Lauren, a special education teacher, parent to Finnian. Michael consistently beats me at ping-pong, just as when he was a boy. One night when he was eight, I stepped into his room to wish him a good night and Michael said, "I'm playing tag with the wind." His room was dark and his chin was on the windowsill beside his bed as the wind rushed through the trees.

"I'll teach you how to jump on the wind's back, and then away we go," Peter Pan said to us all.

I loved reading aloud to the children: *Kittens are Like That*, Richard Scarry books, *Clifford*, *Madeline*, *My Father's Dragon*, and *Treasure Island*.

Each night I gave the children piggyback rides up the stairs. One night I pretended that Michael was Peter Pan as I lifted him up into the air as we sang the Peter Pan song and I placed him first on his bed, then on the dresser, and then on the bookshelf. He loved standing on the bookshelf.

I remember the moment David was born. The nurse whisked him to a small heating tray monitor to regulate his temperature. As David wiggled on his back and cried, I asked the nurse, "Can I touch him?"

"Of course you can touch him," she smiled. "He's your son." I loved playing hide-and-seek with David in the tire park by the grammar school.

When I hugged David as he prepared to leave for the airport, I couldn't say the word "goodbye." Peter Pan's author reminds us, "Never say goodbye because goodbye means going away and going away means forgetting."

Perhaps I am the child left behind. I want to go ice-skating with my brothers and sisters again. I want to go back. I want to go on the sailboat with my father and sit beside my mother as she tells me about Peter Rabbit and her childhood in Belgium.

I want to sleep in the tree fort with my brother all over again and bake apples with him in the woods. I want to inhale the autumn aroma of burning leaves as my father rakes the driveway once again. I want to color Easter eggs with my children.

I am an aging Baby Boomer and I still love climbing trees, hunting for salamanders, eating Cracker Jacks, and riding bikes with my sister. I'd like to go trick-or-treating again and hunting for chocolate eggs this Easter. The author of *Peter Pan* famously wrote, "All children, except one, grow up." Perhaps life is all a fantasy.

Where is long ago? In what sandbox; from which star?

SPRING

I enjoy the spring more than the autumn now.
One does, I think, as one gets older.
—VIRGINIA WOOLF, *Jacob's Room*

O ne spring, when my son was a little boy, he came rushing into the house to announce to his mother and me like a town crier, "The crocuses are out! The crocuses are out!" and in his hand he had gathered a small bunch of healthy, vigorous purple crocuses that proved, once again, that spring had arrived.

We all look forward to this jolt of attention, to this new season of hope. The woodchuck wakes up from under the shed. The tree blossoms and flowers remember their former selves that are once again reborn. One of my favorite poets, Rainer Maria Rilke, wrote, "It is spring again. The earth is like a child that knows poems by heart."

Robins seem to haul in spring on their wings. They do not return because of the heat; they return because of the food source. Bugs and worms pop up again from the ground. The robins change their diet in winter to fruit, so they fly south, but when the air starts to climb out of the thirties and forties the birds reclaim their place in the yard and lord over our sentiments for love or courage, and for our joy that we can sit outside again with a book and a glass of iced tea.

In many ways, spring is not really a place, but an idea, like *Brigadoon* (the Alan Jay Lerner musical), that entranced village that wakes up every hundred years for one day, a one-day season of life, like spring, and then the time is up, the blossoms disappear, and the buds on the trees are transformed into summer leaves, and spring, like *Brigadoon*, closes once again.

In May the grass, like dormant ballet dancers, lift its blade-like arms to the sun and sways to the recognizable aroma released from the soil's bacteria reacting to the new moisture and heat.

Spring means baseball when many of us dream of being a center fielder, or yearn for a hotdog and beer at the stadium. As we buy some peanuts and Cracker Jacks, a day at the park is like spring, makes us feel there is only one day, one season, and we don't care if we never go back to our work and sorrows, or to the cold days of winter.

I remember speaking with my grandmother as she sat on the back porch with a sprig of yellow forsythia in her hands. She looked at each stem, admired each gold floret, looked at me, smiled, and said, "I am so glad I have another spring."

Even the change of the time on our clocks suggests the personality of the equinox: spring ahead, fall back. We feel this urge to spring ahead when the sun tips beyond the equator to our favor and increases the length of the days and the temperature of the air as we spin towards summer, and we fall back in autumn accepting that the confines of winter are near. I am glad for another spring that comes in like a lamb.

Kobayashi Issa (1772–1858), the great Japanese poet, wrote, "What a strange thing! To be alive beneath the cherry blossoms." Such a privilege to be alive, to inhale the aromas of March, to hear the return of the songbirds, and to sit beneath the cherry blossoms.

Spring, the Brigadoon of seasons. The crocuses are out! The crocuses are out! Plant some peas.

BUGS, BUGS, AND MORE BUGS

Any foolish boy can stamp on a beetle, but all the
professors in the world cannot make a beetle.
—ARTHUR SCHOPENHAUER

Last Monday I made my way downstairs to feed the cat, and then
walked to the side door to retrieve the morning paper from the
driveway. Suddenly I saw a slight movement on the baseboard in
the mud room. Too early for ants, I thought. When I looked closer, I
saw it was a small bug, just a bug. I scooped it up with a bit of paper,
opened the backdoor, and tossed it outside.

On Tuesday morning when I made my way downstairs to feed the cat,
and walked to the side door to retrieve the paper, I saw ten or twenty small
bugs crawling on the baseboard in the mud room. "It's an invasion!" The
good Samaritan in me abandoned my compassion and I swatted them,
stomped them, grabbed paper towels, and wiped up the mess.

Bugs. Bugs. Where were they coming from? I checked the downstairs
bathroom. Clean. I ran down to the basement to check the beams and
crevasses. No bugs. I looked inside the storage closet in the mudroom.
Nothing.

When there were carpenter ants, I called the exterminator, and we
had no more carpenter ants. When there was a huge bee's nest in the
attic, I called the exterminator. No more bees. I didn't see the need

to call anyone on Tuesday because I had cleared up all the bugs and there couldn't possibly be anymore.

Well! This morning there were bugs on the baseboards, in the mudroom, on the walls, on the ceiling, and crawling on the floor.

In China, the dragonfly is looked upon as a spiritual guide. Ladybugs bring luck. If a butterfly lands next to you, it suggests that you are coming close to a transformation in your spirit, or that you will be changing jobs, or you will have a revelation of who you are. The American Indians thought that the spider wove the web of creation. Bees represent hard work. My bugs represented an invasion of the Huns, creatures that are determined to lift up my house and carry it off to bug heaven. Yikes!

I once again cleaned up the bugs, sprayed the walls, and wiped up the mess with paper towels. Where were these creatures coming from? I was determined to stay up all night to and see if I could find the source of my trouble.

Ah!

The snow in the yard is melting quickly, but the birds still depend on me for seeds. Blue jays, juncos, cardinals, turtle doves, starlings, the nuthatch, they all provide us with the dance of life in their plumage, with the excitement of their flights to the birdfeeder, with their entertaining activities as they peck, hop, and flutter.

This morning, when I looked out the window, I saw that the birdfeeder was empty. I walked into the *clean,* bug-free mudroom, opened the storage closet, and reached in for the half-filled bag of birdseed and carried it outside.

I inhaled the fresh morning air. I saw the cardinal in a distant bush. I unhooked the green birdfeeder, placed in on the ground, lifted the top and picked up the birdseed bag. Holding it in my hands, leaning over close to the top of the birdfeeder, when I poured the seeds . . . BUGS! BUGS! I mean BUGS! There seemed to be more bugs then seeds. I looked inside the bag and it seemed as if the contents were alive. The seeds appeared to be moving, pulsing, and twirling. It was my own miniature horror movie. I dropped the bag, ran into the house, and grabbed a thick, black garbage bag from under the sink. I ran back outside, picked up the bug infested birdseed, dropped it into the trash bag, dumped it in the trash barrel, and dragged the barrel to the road.

I bought a new bag of seeds, opened it to make sure that there were no bugs, and filled the birdfeeder. The birds are happy. I am happy. There were no more bugs in the mudroom.

I appreciate what the German philosopher Schopenhauer once said about bugs: "Any foolish boy can stamp on a beetle, but all the professors in the world cannot make a beetle."

I get that, the extraordinary creation of the simplest creature, but just the same I was glad to see the sanitation department arrive with their truck. I felt a great satisfaction as their hydraulic jaw swallowed that bag of bugs, and I was pleased to see the garbage truck grind off into the far distance and disappear.

STUBBORN SPRING

You can cut all the flowers
but you cannot keep Spring from coming.

—PABLO NERUDA

I am reminded about the extraordinary advances that technology has added to our lives.

We now talk into our wrist watches as Dick Tracy did in the comics. I do not have to cut down trees, split logs, and stoke the fireplace. Instead, I just listen to the hum of the furnace in the basement.

In the seventeenth and eighteenth centuries lamps were filled with whale oil. The whale was killed, blubber stripped from the carcass and boiled. The ooze was transported to villages for sale in the local mercantile stores, and then people poured the oil into their lamps, lit the wick, and voila: light in the cabin. Today I just flick a switch and the room is illuminated.

I have friends who just say "lights on" and the lamps in the house magically glow.

Automobiles, computers, health care, printing . . . all extraordinary additions to our rich lives. I am startled that for seventy years all I have had to do when I needed water was push a small chrome plated knob and fresh drinking water gushed out of the spout of a slender faucet. No well. No bucket. No trip to the river. No jug on the top of my head.

But with the great conveniences, there is the loss of poetic charm to our lives. Bakers in Belgium specialty shops sell the famous *Couque de Dinant*, a large, hard tan-colored cookie. It is made from equal parts flour and honey. The dough is pressed into the famous wood molds in the shape of fish, or country squires, or a fruit basket, and then it is baked in the oven at 575 degrees until the honey caramelizes. When the cookie cools, it is nearly as hard as wood. You don't bite into it and chew; you break off one small piece at a time and let it slowly melt in your mouth. We always teased at home that a true test to see if someone is Belgian was to give them a *Couque de Dinant* and see if they like the taste and consistency.

My sister made a number of these cookies for the family as Christmas gifts. Mine was in the shape of a large heart. When the microwave was invented, someone in our family placed the cookie inside the magical box and the cookie was no longer hard and it now could be bitten, chewed, and swallowed without any lingering effort.

Poetry is a combination of images and insight, emotions mixed with concrete images. The modern world seems to kill the poetry inside the things we own and the things that we do each day.

We don't use iconic horse and buggies any longer. We don't use simple ink and paper to write letters. We look at a television screen instead of out the window. But, of course, there is a balance between delight and reality.

This morning it was 11 degrees. I sat comfortably on the couch while the baseboard heat maintained an even 70 degrees. My cat, Stuart, was sitting on my lap. I had a cup of hot chocolate on the side table, and I saw a photograph in the paper about the persecution of the Rohingya people in Myanmar: hundreds of starving people with their hands outstretched hoping for food. A mother cradling her dead baby. Fathers carrying their children through the muddied waters of a river.

I can take a *Couque de Dinant* and either soften it in the microwave or break off a piece and let the sweet hard biscuit slowly melt in my mouth.

HOME IS IN THE ARMS OF A LOVER

Arms, take your last embrace!

—WILLIAM SHAKESPEARE, Juliet to her assumed dead Romeo

Three weeks ago, while walking in the historic district of Charleston, South Carolina, I tripped on the cobblestone and fell on my right shoulder. People all around suddenly came to my rescue, asking if I was hurt. I bounced up quickly, brushed my shirt and pants, and said confidently, "I'm okay. Thank you. Really, I am fine." And I was fine, until the next day when my arm ached.

Now when I move my arm in a rotating motion, I hear a little click, and a stabbing pain shoots through my body just below my right shoulder. I thought the pain would subside and the irritation would eventually disappear. It has been three weeks and the pain is still there.

My father's cousin many years ago fell through a plate glass window and the broken glass severed the inside of his left arm to the point where surgery could not make much of a difference, and he suffered the rest of his life with a useless arm and much pain.

My grandfather was shot during World War I and lost the power of his left arm for the rest of his life.

No one knows how the famous statue of the Venus de Milo lost its arms. The statue was discovered in 1820 on the island of Milo in the Aegean Sea. After a farmer and sailor discovered the work, it was sold to France and has been in the Louvre Museum ever since.

What do we need when we are lonely? What do we need when we are sad? What do we need when we feel defeated? An embrace. We need our arms to embrace each other. To bond with another human being in such an intimate way is to let go of our temporal selves and pour our spiritual selves into the presence of the other. By giving ourselves to another human being we release tension, share joy, and communicate our intentions.

In the famous painting *The Return of the Prodigal Son* by Rembrandt, the father is shown embracing his son who was once lost and now was found back in the circle of his father's love and forgiveness.

I also admire Picasso's work called *The Embrace*. The background is a subtle blue; the flesh tones of the two nude lovers are illuminated with light. The woman is pregnant; her head is bent down into the shoulder of the man, her cheek pressed against his face. He too is bowing into her, and her arms are embracing him, tenderly over his shoulders. It can be seen as a sad image, or an image of sudden silence. Something is happening with this couple, but there is no doubt the embrace is intimate and expressing vulnerability.

Or look at Edvard Munch's famous painting *The Kiss*. You cannot see the lovers' faces, but you can see how their arms just lock around each other's bodies with tenderness.

A kiss is often sensual, an embrace is always tender.

In sacred dying we embrace these who inhale and exhale for the last time.

The waltz is a public embrace. The word *waltz* comes from the old German meaning to glide. We glide in the embrace of the other across the dance floor and in such an intimate dance there is the communication of the body from one to the other, the movement, the eyes looking into the eyes, the combination of letting go and holding on.

What is wonderful about the embrace is that no person has more power over the other. Both people have the same ability to exercise a tender hug, and in the embrace of the other we discover missing parts of who we are.

I have an appointment with the doctor on Monday to look at my arm.

POET AS FOX

One runs the risk of weeping a little, if one lets oneself be tamed . . .
—ANTOINE DE SAINT-EXUPÉRY

If you ask a novelist where she writes, she will tell you she writes at a desk, or in her room, or she will say that she writes in a tavern, or on the backs of envelopes. If you ask a poet where he writes he might tell you that he writes in the shadows of rocks, inside the cracks in granite, curled up like a dying fox.

A poet is familiar with the weight of stones and the spirit in the stones. He will, like Michelangelo, want to cut away into the marble to find his Pietà, or his David. The shadows that haunt a poet are the shadows of his past, the images of the women he has loved, the texture of sand on his feet, the memories of bluebonnets in spring.

A poet likes to squeeze inside the granite of life, finding that small crack in the hard stone where he can expand, be unlike the stone, and be more like the moisture of life that seeps in between the rules of living. A novelist might say that she is like a hawk surveying the world before she strikes; a poet says he is like the fox, curled inside the dark place, eager to find the light of the morning sun.

A poet resists the confines of walls in his life, rejects the rules of the public, and lives according to the rules of his emotions. This is not a temporary place. He is born with this nature, this sensual response to color and sound, and as he matures, he tries to create a symphony with words, or tries to sculpt a woman from a block of stone. The novelist stacks one story upon another until the weight defines a reality. The poet scatters images and sounds across the page until reality dissolves into dreams.

A poet sometimes thinks of himself as a little god, or what a little god might be. He feels at times alone among ferns and bison. The poet swims with the whales. The novelist gives the whales names.

A poet learns to be merciful, accepts that the roots of plants do not bleed as we bleed. The poet tastes honey on her tongue. The novelist shows no mercy, grinds the world into dust, and eats with a fork and knife.

Ask a novelist how she writes, and she will say in a straight line from beginning to end. Ask a poet how he writes, and he will say that we are born to follow the circle, to trace the shape of the moon with our desires.

The poet wants to know the purpose of the circle at Stonehenge, balance his intimate world at the tip of a pen, and trace where he has been with his evening prayers.

I know where I have been. I have left footprints in the sand at the ocean shore.

I spent the afternoon with my mother and her company: my niece with her four children from Massachusetts. They may as well have been ambassadors from the regal land of faraway loveliness. The children colored eggs for Easter. We all rushed to the window to admire the twelve wild turkeys that moved through the garden from left to right in a procession of forest royalty. I held the youngest child in my arms. He looked at me and smiled. When he is thirty, I will be ninety-six, the age of my mother.

What does the poet see in the wild turkeys and in the eyes of a nine-month-old child? Shadows of the future? Are the things that the poet sees just illusions?

Ask a novelist how she ends the day, and she might say with a glass of wine, or reading Twain or Dickens. Ask a poet how he ends the day, and he might say pulling his knees to his chest, crossing his arms around his body, and sliding back into the shadows, back into the womb, back into the den of the closing dusk stroking his dry lips with a soft finger.

JACK-IN-THE-BOX

I am lonely, lonely.
I was born to be lonely,
I am best so!
—WILLIAM CARLOS WILLIAMS

What is hidden from the eyes waits in secret; what is reveled abandons magic. I, for one, believed nuns possessed all sorts of magic. I spent six years in Catholic grammar school and was, from the beginning, enthralled with the nuns' black and white habits.

I was raised with Dominican Sisters, and when I first met my first-grade teacher, I was afraid Sister Elizabeth Anne didn't have any arms or hair. She was standing at the door with her arms crossed in the folds of her habit, and of course, in 1958 we never saw a nun's hair. Her head was completely covered with a black veil; her beautiful face was framed in a coif, that headpiece worn for modesty.

What I liked best about their habits were the secret pockets. I watched as Sister Elizabeth Anne walked up and down the aisles, and if a boy didn't have a pencil, she slipped her hand under her tunic, fiddled around, and produced a long, yellow number two pencil with a perfect point. I watched her during the year pull out handkerchiefs, a watch, a ruler, erasers, chalk. I would not have been surprised if she eventually produced a giraffe or a balloon from deep within the hidden cloth of her flowing robe.

I liked that: something hidden with the sudden moment of "Ah ha!"

I still like the jack-in-the box. There is a tin box in my memory no bigger than a toaster. The box was covered with elephants and tigers. There was a small, metal crank at the side and a red knob. When the crank was turned, there was that famous plunking music "Pop Goes the Weasel." Each time I sang the famous little song:

> All around the mulberry bush,
> the monkey chased the weasel,
> the weasel thought it was all in fun,
> pop goes the weasel.

In England, in the mid-1800s there began a popular dance called "Pop Goes the Weasel." As was reported in the *Suffolk Chronicle* in Ipswich, England, on December 18, 1852, "a country dance, entitled 'Pop Goes the Weasel', one of the most mirth inspiring dances which can well be imagined." I always liked to image the clown hidden deep inside the tin box, and when the music turned just at the exact moment, POP, the clown leaped out of the box with his smiling face and funny hat.

Is there a cruel clown hidden inside the sorrows of the world mocking us as it leaps out of the box with a spring in its belly? Does Sister Elizabeth Anne have a magic wand that she could wave over our heads as a blessing that will protect us?

This morning as I entered the living room after a restless night, I saw a long, rectangular pearl-blue light bathing the living room floor. I wasn't expecting the moon at 5:00 in the morning. I didn't know it was hidden behind the trees, up in the morning sky, looking down on us with its light.

Could Sister Elizabeth Anne hide the moonlight in her black and white robe and produce the light whenever her students were afraid, lonely, lost in the chaos of their thoughts that they do not understand?

Last night I sprawled out on my bed as the moonlight bathed me, covered me with all its power. No one knows I slept with the moon. No one knows of my hidden self, curled up deep within the tin box of my house. No one knows that I am the jack-in-the box waiting for someone to crank the handle and sing before my arrival. No one knows that I stepped out of the tin box and swam nude in the moonlight.

We have a public self and a hidden self. We are people who dress, work, mingle with the crowd, and we are people with hidden lives, swimming with the whales in the moonlight, dreaming about the music we hear, always hoping someone will find us curled in the tin box waiting to set us free into the blue waters of who we truly are.

BEAUTY FOUND

Her kimono stood out from her neck, and her back and shoulders
were like a white fan spread under it. There was something sad
about the full flesh under that white powder. It suggested a woolen
cloth, and again it suggested the pelt of some animal.
        —Yasunari Kawabata, *Snow Country*

Do you hunt for treasure? In the woods behind the old house
where I grew up there was an abandoned trash pit against a small
hill. In the early 1900s there was no garbage collection, so people
burned their rubbish, or buried it. By the time my family moved in,
trucks hauled our garbage away on a regular basis, but the old garbage
pit in the woods remained, and it was a grand day when we discovered
this archaeological treasure trove of artifacts from an earlier time: chips
of porcelain plates with blue flowers, rusted cans, green and blue
bottles. My sisters and brothers and I thought that these discoveries
were rare and valuable. Of course, they were not; but to children on an
adventure, these things were pirates' booty and kings' gold.

Remember how excited Jem and Scott were in *To Kill a Mockingbird*
when they found a medal, a watch, and two soap carvings of a boy
and girl? We all like that feeling of discovering a favorite antique, red
dress, book, painting, or lost piece of jewelry.

Last summer, while we were visiting our daughter in Portland,
Oregon, Karen suggested that we visit Powell's Bookstore, which is

considered the largest independently owned bookstore in the world. I jumped at the chance, for I was sure to find a treasure. And I did: a large, boxed set of fourteen Japanese colored wood-engravings with a book that offered a brief history of wood-engraving and information about each print.

One of my favorites is #2 by Suzuki Harunobu. This print is about a "kneeling youth who, while admiring a bird in a cage, is handing over a love-letter to his girl." I learned that Harunobu was born in 1725 and died in 1770. He was the first one to create full-color wood-engraving prints, and he was the most famous wood-engraving artist during his lifetime.

In the background of the print are cherry blossoms, a wonderful season to offer your lover a note. A young woman is sitting in the middle of the room wearing a powder-blue garment that drapes to the floor. There is a brown birdcage on her lap, and in the cage a gray and white bird. The woman's lover is kneeling before her. He has a black sword hanging from his left side; his robe is brown, and his uses his left hand to tuck his letter under the cage so that the girl will find it when she lifts the cage from her lap.

What made Harunobu's work famous, besides the color techniques he mastered, were the subjects he chose for his art. Up until that time, the artists used emperors, folklore, and legends as their subjects. Harunobu used scenes from everyday life: a girl jumping, the moon rising, potted trees in the snow, street vendors, women combing their hair. He found treasured images in the ordinary world.

I have learned in my own writing where the treasures lie: my own chips of blue porcelain, green bottles, soap carvings, and cherry blossoms. The poet William Carlos Williams wrote, "No ideas but in things." What he meant was that we find much power in poetry in objects around us rather than in the abstract, academic skeletons of theories and philosophies. Instead of writing a poem about loneliness, write as a lonely man and describe the moss on the side of a tree. Instead of writing about love, be in love and write about slipping a letter under a birdcage that sits on the lap of your lover.

Here is a little poem that I wrote that is all about admiring a woman. It doesn't use the word "admire" or "love" or "sex" or "desire." Those are abstract ideas. Instead, the poem defines the qualities of a kimono: the long fabric, the brocade, the sleeves, the sash, the obi. The poem doesn't say that beauty is often best appreciated from a distance or from the hint of beauty as the woman stands alone while a single heron flies off into the moonlight. Do we abandon beauty? Do you let beauty bathe in the moonlight undisturbed?

KIMONO

There is no meaning of the word kimono
Without you standing inside the long fabric
Colored with thick brocade of russet leaves
Or plum blossoms, butterflies or bamboo.

There is no meaning without the hem
Falling to your small ankles and the

Robe wrapped around your body,
The left side of the flowers
Over the right.

The collar has no meaning without the
Contour of your silken neck,
And the wide sleeves are empty husks
Without the movement of your arms.

I have seen the sash of the bright kimono
Tied to the back, but in place of the obi
Let it be my arms in a tight embrace
Around your waist.

As the white heron pulls in
The evening moon.

I have always admired Japanese wood-engravings: the movement of a fan, the sensual fins of a goldfish, the powerful white foam of the ocean waves, the tilt of a woman's head. There is an order, a sense of well-being in the images of hairpins, the river cranes, the mountains capped in snow that distinguishes the formal art of Japan as unique and beautiful.

A treasure can be a bauble made of paste or useless tin; it can be planet earth in a dance-like spin, but for me the best treasures are the outstretched hands in greeting from people whom I love.

INSPIRATION DOESN'T KNOCK, BUT WHISPERS

It is in the night, the middle seam,
Where the folds of inspiration stitch my dreams.
—CHRISTOPHER DE VINCK

Many years ago, I was sitting in the Morris Country Library in Morristown, New Jersey. Morristown was first inhabited by the Lenni Lenape Native Americans for 6,000 years; it is the county seat. It was the headquarters of George Washington during the revolution for independence.

It was also the place where Augusta and her naughty cat, Trab, were born. Let me explain.

During those years I was working at a production company that wanted to create a children's television program, and they wanted it to include children's books and the essentials of reading. I was in the library to do a little research on children's television, and to look up the history of reading education in the United States.

I remember sitting at one of the tables, feeling scholarly beside the pile of books I had pulled from the shelves. Before me was a yellow legal pad for note-taking, my pen, and my eagerness to find the secrets of good television and good children's literature.

Then a little girl's voice popped into my head and I began to write spontaneously . . .

If you think enough fanciful thoughts something good is bound to happen. One night I thought very hard that a peach tree would grow in our back lot under the moonlight and that the next day I would pick the fruit and bake a pie. I like the crust.

Just like that, Augusta was born, a ten-year-old girl who lost her mother to cancer, whose father was a veterinarian, and who had a hole in her heart that she tried to fill with her good cheer and with adventures with her cat, Trab. Trab liked jungles and chocolate, and he whined a lot, and preferred to be curled up next to the fireplace rather than roam the world chasing pirates and giant cats. Three months later my book *Augusta and Trab* was complete, and it was published the following year.

What a pleasure it was creating that book.

It is easier for me, now, to conjure up a place, a character, and a starting point from which to write. I have been doing this for a half-century. But there were just two moments in my life where I did not have to massage the muse with preliminary music or reading. Only twice was I hit with what people call inspiration: when I first began to write poetry, and when I wrote those first two pages of that little novel in the library.

In the book, lonely Augusta meets Hildamore, an old soothsayer, a universal woman, a Mother Goose, a magical guide from the woods of our sorrows and fears. Hildamore asks Augusta, "Are you lost?" And the girl replies:

"Well, something doesn't seem right inside. . . .

"But I am brave. I can stand on a tall ship in a nasty storm. I am willing to slide into a strange, pink shell. I can walk through dark shadows, under thick vines, and along green moss. But sometimes I feel as I am just a broken leaf floating from a branch in autumn. I feel like an icicle fallen from the eaves of a roof. I feel as if I am a lost balloon carried away wherever the wind chooses."

So Hildamore guides the girl to a huge bookshelf, selects a large book and places it on the girl's lap.

I bent over the book as if I were looking for a telephone number, and flipped the pages here and there. Hildamore leaned over my shoulder and ran her crooked finger along one page until she stopped at a line. "Read."

"Love is strong as death," I read.

"And now here," Hildamore continued, pointing at another line. So again I read.

"Your mother raised you up under the apple tree." But I didn't understand.

"Read," Hildamore answered with another pointing of her finger.

"Who is this that comes up from the wilderness?" Then I asked, "Me?"

Hildamore nodded with a smile. "Here, Augusta. Read here."

"Many waters cannot quench love," and then I thought about the sea and the pink shell and the rain I like to walk under without an umbrella.

"And here, Augusta."

"Awake, O north wind; and come, blow upon my garden," and I thought about the yarrow that Max and I picked so long ago.

"Millie."

"The flowers appear on the earth; the time of the singing of birds is come, and the voice of the turtle is heard in our land."

"It will all be of use to you someday, Augusta. Now read here."

"'I am the rose of Sharon and the lily of the valley,' I like that," I said.

At the end, Augusta knows all over again who she is. We find ourselves in books: our courage on the raft with Huckleberry Finn, our love in *Dr. Zhivago*, our fears and joys in *The Christmas Carol*.

Jack London, one of my favorite short story writers, wrote in an essay, *Getting into Print*, "Don't loaf and invite inspiration; light after it with a club." Inspiration doesn't knock, but whispers.

TRUE POWER

Nearly all men can stand adversity,
but if you want to test a man's character, give him power.
—ABRAHAM LINCOLN

ast month I was invited to give a talk at Boston College about the theology of the disabled, a talk based on my brother's disabilities and how families tend to both the sorrow and joy of seemingly broken people in their lives.

We are a broken world community. The uneven distribution of wealth and food leaves millions of people starving to death. The planet is being choked with fumes. Truth is manipulated, and art is degraded into popular vulgarities.

I feel that we human beings are constantly picking up the broken sticks and branches in the back yard of the world and trying to maintain beauty and order.

Before my talk I had a bit of time to walk around Brookline, a town created in the seventeenth century by European colonists after displacing the Algonquian tribes that lived there for centuries.

I looked into the windows of the jewelry shops and restaurants. I admired the hundred-year-old homes and office buildings, and then I came upon a small sign: *John F. Kennedy National Historic Site ¼ mile.* I had no idea what the site was, so out of curiosity I made a left on Beals Street and continued walking. Such a beautiful tree-lined street. Each house was an American gem: three stories, each house different, each painted in calm pastels, or in elegant grays or blues.

After my quarter-mile walk I came upon a house to my right: 83 Beals Street, and to the right of the front door was a bold sign:

National Park Service: U.S. Department of the Interior
John Fitzgerald Kennedy
National Historic Site
Birthplace of America's 35th President

The house only opens for tours from May to October, so I was not able to stand inside the bedroom where President Kennedy was born. But standing in front of the house gave me a moment to pause. Here I was at the site where JFK's life began on May 29, 1917. I have also visited Dealey Plaza in Dallas where he died on November 22, 1963, and I have stood at the base of his grave and seen the perpetual flame in Arlington Cemetery.

I was twelve when President Kennedy died. I was sitting in my seventh-grade English class, right next to the teacher's desk taking a spelling test. When the vice-principal stepped into the room and leaned over, I heard him whisper into the teacher's ear, "The President was shot." Soon after, school was closed early, and I walked home.

I didn't know death when I was twelve. I didn't know politics, war, evil, or suffering. Mine was a childhood filled with brothers and sisters, Creamsicles in summer, and sleigh riding in winter.

My mother and father taught us that my blind, disabled, intellectually void brother was not a pile of broken sticks, but a spiritually whole tree of life and uniquely himself. Oliver began his life in Brussels, Belgium, and thirty-two years later he died in my mother's arms in New Jersey. He's buried at the Benedictine Priory in Weston, Vermont. There is no perpetual flame at his grave, but these perpetual words are engraved in his tombstone: "Blessed are the pure of heart for they shall see God."

On May 8, 1963, President Kennedy said to a group of foreign students: "The ancient Greek definition of happiness was the full use of your powers along the lines of excellence." The motto of Boston College is "always be excellent." We who wish to improve the world strive for excellence with the limited or limitless powers that we possess.

WANTING TO BE LIKED

When people laugh at Mickey Mouse, it's because he's so human;
and that is the secret of his popularity.
—WALT DISNEY

When I was in high school, I found on the floor a neatly folded piece of paper in the shape of a triangle, and I knew what it meant: someone had dropped a note from a friend. I remember stooping down and surreptitiously picking it up . . . and pretending that it was for me. I was a lonely teenager, filled with those universal insecurities of odd hair, crooked teeth, gangly arms, and no concept of algebra or girls, so I created different fantasies that filled in the gaps.

In the magazine *Popular Mechanics* there was an advertisement for a Benson Helicopter, a kit that promised quick assembly and a true flying experience within sixty days. It was my plan, carried out countless times in my imagination, to buy the kit, use my father's tools, build the helicopter, and fly over the high school just when the yellow buses snaked along the wide driveway up to the brick building.

It was my plan to land the helicopter on the front grass, step out, and walk in the halls all day with my pilot's helmet tucked under my arm the way the football quarterback did each time he stepped off the field at the end of a game.

Realizing that I did not even know the difference between a Phillips head screwdriver and a flathead screwdriver, I switched my fantasy to a 1929 DeSoto. I figured I'd buy my popularity-making machine already built and ready to go.

Bill, one of my classmates, owned a beautiful DeSoto sporting those large, owl-eyed headlights. The antique automobile was a squared sedan, a jewel of a car that everyone noticed when Bill drove into the student parking lot. When I sheepishly asked Bill where he got his car, he said something about money, and working on it himself. I didn't have money and, as I said, the Phillips head was not my friend.

As I stumbled through high school, I realized that the popular boys owned these black jackets with white sleeves. Their names were embroidered on the left side, and the back had bright patches of footballs or tennis rackets. Ah, that is all I had to do. Buy one of those jackets and I'd be liked.

Of course, when I stepped into the school store and asked the coach about ordering a jacket, he looked down at me skeptically and asked, "What is your varsity sport?" The word "varsity" sat in the corner of my naive mind beside the screwdrivers. I had no idea what "varsity" meant, and when he waved his hand and said, "You can buy this other coat," I slinked out of the store in my crummy jeans and rumpled shirt.

Because my campaign to be liked wasn't working, I made up friends: the cheerleader who might wave to me as she called out a cheer at a basketball game; the smart chemistry student who might ask me for help with an equation.

And then I found that note on the floor. I didn't dare read it immediately; instead, I stuck it into my pocket as I was herded with all the other kids to history class. Only on my way home while walking under the railroad trestle did I dare open it. "I think he's cute!!," it read. The penmanship was made with soft curls and elongated swoops. The ink was blue. The exclamation point, bold and doubled. I wanted to be a double exclamation point in a girl's eyes when I was in high school, so I just pretended that this note clearly represented one girl's opinion conveyed to another that, indeed, Chris was cute (double exclamation point). For months I flew this girl in my Benson Helicopter as she held onto my waist like girls do to guys on a motorcycle.

I drove my imaginary girlfriend to the prom in a 1929 DeSoto at least fifty times, and loaned her my varsity football jacket over and over again as I imagined hearing her voice cooing in the dark, "I'm cold." Girls cooed in my imagination.

In high school I wanted to be liked, and popular, but I always felt as if I was that famous square peg trying to fit into that round hole. I didn't realize at the time that a Phillips head screwdriver wouldn't help with the mechanics of maturity.

MONSTERS

"Hallo, Rabbit," he said, "is that you?"
"Let's pretend it isn't," said Rabbit, "and see what happens."
—A. A. MILNE

Do you remember Maurice Sendak's famous children's book *Where the Wild Things Are?* How Max, angry and unhappy, dressed in his wolf costume, was transported to a mythical place where he met up with monsters that ". . . roared their terrible roars and gnashed their terrible teeth and rolled their terrible eyes and showed their terrible claws." It is a story about a boy projecting his fears and anger onto these four creatures with horns, claws, sharp teeth, and hidden charm. Max overwhelms the beasts and they make him king.

Are we the king of our monsters? Do we dress in a wolf costume to pretend that we are fierce when we leave our homes in the morning for the day's challenges?

Do we surround ourselves with things we fear and then conquer them one by one in the jungle of our imaginations? How we respond to the joys and sorrows in our lives determines the type of people we are.

Last fall I planted fifty tulip bulbs in my back garden. I liked the feel of the bulbs in my hand: packed energy in the mysterious roots, the potential flowers aching to blossom in the spring.

After the maple and oak trees shed their autumn leaves and shivered in the winter, after the ground began to thaw in the early spring, I walked into the yard each day to see if there was any progress with my tulips. Nothing. Nothing . . . and then those first green tips broke through the warm soil.

Day after day there was more evidence of the thriving plants: first thumb-sized shoots, then slender leaves. I felt accomplished, king of the garden! Look at my treasure! Soon the flowers will prove I am a great gardener. Look what I have done! And then, *WHAM!*

One night a monster invaded my garden. Every tulip plant was eaten down to a nub of chewed, ragged tiny stumps of disappointment. I wanted to roar my terrible roars. Max swung in Sendak's imagination from the trees with his monster. I wanted to dress in a wolf costume and chase down whatever ate my tulip plants. I was convinced it was the deer, but I didn't notice any deer droppings. There are no groundhogs in my yard, no bears, tigers, crocodiles, flying monkeys from the Wizard of Oz.

With each passing day I developed in my mind a profile of this fiend, this ogre, this dragon, this tulip-eater ravishing my Eden. I was determined to catch the beast in the act and fling it down to monster purgatory.

For the next few days, each time before I went to bed, I flicked on the floodlights and illuminated the backyard. One night, nothing. The next night the neighbor walking his dog on the street. The third night a dark movement at the end of the yard, a slow movement . . . ah ha!

A rabbit! A rabbit eating what was left of the tulips! I was angry, filled with hostility, ready to be Elmer Fudd with my rifle and chase that wascally wabbit out of my garden. But then I watched the rabbit: his ears pointed, the classic, silent movement of his legs, and I thought about that wonderful play *Harvey*, written by Mary Chase about Elwood P. Dowd, an eccentric man who imagines he befriends a six-foot rabbit. Elwood's family of course thinks Elwood is crazy, but we in the audience come to believe in this mythical companion.

At one point Elwood says, "In this world, you must be oh so smart, or oh so pleasant. Well, for years I was smart. I recommend pleasant." The tulip monster in my yard turned out to be a two-pound brown rabbit. Tulips invaded our country by way of sixteenth-century Turkey and Central Asia. Holland accelerated the world's interest in these colorful perennials, but the rabbits were here first.

Instead of chasing the rabbit from the yard, I unzipped and stepped out of my wolf costume, closed the floodlights, and said aloud, "Okay, Harvey. Enjoy the tulips." And then the monster disappeared from my anger.

Part Five
ORDINARY
AND
EXTRAORDINARY

IT WAS A BEAUTIFUL DAY IN THE NEIGHBORHOOD

Towns are like people. Old ones often have character,
the new ones are interchangeable.
—WALLACE STEGNER, *Angel of Repose*

T he hall light bulb is out," my wife said. "Maybe you could go to Jones' and buy—oh . . . that's right. The hardware store is gone."

Not only is the hardware store closed for good, but America at the moment seems to be closing. Robbie Jones was the proprietor of his grandfather's and father's hardware store that began business in 1929. And Robbie and his family lived in the house that was connected to the store for more than forty-three years.

For the half-century that I have lived in Pompton Plains, New Jersey, Robbie was always here. In the summer the door to the store was always open. In the winter there was a Norman Rockwell feel about stepping inside onto the wood floors, feeling the heat, stomping the snow off our shoes, and seeing Robbie at the end of the aisle behind the counter among hanging tools.

During Hurricane Sandy, credit cards didn't work and people didn't have cash, but they needed urgent supplies, so Robbie opened his store and told people to help themselves and pay later.

Robbie was a volunteer firefighter, a father, a husband, Santa Claus on the fire engine that wove its way through the town streets in December from house to house. His daughter babysat for my three children; his two sons were policemen in town.

A place, a town, is made up of past history and present players on the stage walking to the Dutch Reformed Church on Sunday morning, sitting in the yellow school buses pulling up to the high school, swimming at the town lake, sprawling out on the blankets under the Fourth of July fireworks. Robbie's son Jeff said, "Everybody who has grown up in this community has a story that somehow comes back to Jones' Hardware. There is a little piece of it in everybody."

The original building was constructed in 1818. People joke that the hardware store was the second town hall. I thought of it as a second therapist's office where I and most everyone could tell Robbie about their sorrows and joys, and there was always a kind word in return, good advice, or a wise chuckle. James Baldwin once wrote, "Perhaps home is not a place but simply an irrevocable condition."

For eighty-nine years my little community thought that part of the irrevocable condition was Jones' Hardware Store, but then suddenly, all within two miles, new America encroached upon the little blue store: Home Depot, Lowe's, Target, and Walmart. Robbie said his store suddenly became an afterthought. If Home Depot or Lowe's didn't have it, they would come to his place. Robbie's business fell quickly by thirty-five percent, according to his estimate, and his costs doubled. New America was swallowing up yet another old-world jewel.

Remember in John Steinbeck's novel *The Grapes of Wrath* how the Great Depression swallowed up the small farms as big business and the banks combined the land and were more interested in the growth of profits than they were in the growth of corn and communities? America is built on profit, but when money becomes the bedrock of a community, people in the community don't care any longer about the names of their neighbors.

The store is now closed. Robbie and his family are gone. The store, the house, the barn will soon be torn down and replaced with, sigh . . . a bank.

ROMAN HOLIDAY

Veni, vidi, vici. (I came, I saw, I conquered.)
—WILLIAM SHAKESPEARE, *Julius Caesar*

I 've only been to the Vatican once, at the invitation of the Pontifical Council for the Family, to deliver a talk about my disabled brother, Oliver. The Roman Catholic Church was hosting an international conference on the issues of the disabled and how we all should tend to the weakest among us with dignity and compassion. I was asked to give the closing speech.

As I boarded my plane, a fellow passenger jokingly asked when I told him my destination, "And you're going to meet the pope?" I was delighted to say, "Well, yes. I actually am."

When I arrived at the airport in Rome, I was greeted by a charming Italian priest who insisted on carrying my bag. "Welcome," he said. "Welcome to Rome. I am born here. We love you. Come. I take you. We love you come to Roma."

As we entered Vatican City the young priest pulled up before a new building. "It is all beautiful, the trees, the garden. Beautiful. This is the home of the cardinals who live here in Vatican, is where others stay when they elect new pope, or come for conference. Enjoy. Welcome. God loves you."

After the priest explained where my room was, he gave me a small, pink paper and said, "You go wherever you like in the Vatican. When you leave, this is your pass to be let back in." I thanked the priest, and just before he stepped out of the building, he turned and said with a wave, "Peace be with you. God is good."

So there I was in my room, in the shadows of St. Peter's Basilica, unpacking, when I realized I had no camera film. (This was decades ago!) Film. Where can I buy film in the Vatican?

I took the elevator, entered the Vatican gardens, and walked around aimlessly. Cardinals bowed in hello. I bowed. I didn't have the heart to ask if they knew where I could buy film. This was, after all, the home of Michelangelo's *Pietà*, the tombs of the great popes, and the bones of St. Peter. Centuries of holy intrigue crossed the surface of the cobblestones. I just wanted film.

Suddenly I saw to the right of the basilica an open archway in the Vatican's wall, and beyond St. Peter's Square, the streets of Rome.

As I approached the doorway I stopped and noticed hundreds of people standing behind a rope and taking pictures. I stood in the archway and waved. More pictures were taken. I bowed, and then I stepped outside the door and saw to my right and left two Swiss Guards standing at attention. The people were snapping pictures of the guards in their colorful costumes, not some dopey tourist from New Jersey, so I walked toward the rope, and suddenly the people parted. I bowed a few times, waved, and kept walking.

I found a store with film, and as I made my way back across St. Peter's Square, I said to myself, "How am I going to get back in?" Vatican City is completely surrounded by a wall. Ah. My pink pass.

As I approached a new crowd taking pictures, I wiggled up front, and when I stepped over the rope, the people gasped. I boldly walked toward the two Swiss Guards, pulled out my pink pass, and then, as I entered the open doorway, they saluted me. I saluted back.

I did this three times that day. The door. The parting of the crowd. The pink pass. The salutes. The last time, just as I entered the door to the Vatican, I turned, faced the crowd and blessed them as I had seen my parish priest do many times, waving my hand up and down in the sign of the cross. How can that hurt? A New Jersey blessing.

Oh, and I did deliver the speech. I was given a personal introduction to Pope John Paul II. I kissed his ring. He blessed me. I visited the Sistine Chapel, the crypt of the former popes. I was given a tour of the catacombs and the streets of Rome. I was privileged to walk among the grand props of history for a few days mixed in with the happy priest who loved God and made people feel welcome in his city, "My Roma."

ORDINARY AND EXTRAORDINARY

And above all, watch with glittering eyes the whole world around you because the greatest secrets are always hidden in the most unlikely places. Those who don't believe in magic will never find it.
—ROALD DAHL

What appears to be ordinary can hide the extraordinary. Each morning my wife and I take a forty-five-minute stroll to the coffee shop, and on our way we walk through the cemetery. I like looking at the common names: Webb, Manderville, Johnson, and there, our neighbor Grace Robertson. Perfect name for her: "Grace." For years she and I shared stories over the fence about our children, and about the success of the daffodils in the garden.

Grace was many years older than I, her children already grown. She worked over at the high school and enjoyed watching me out her window while I played in the sandbox with my children. And it was humble Grace who changed my life.

"Chris," she said one afternoon as I was raking the leaves, "your name was mentioned as a candidate to be the English department chairman at the high school." I was startled. I didn't know anyone at the local high school. I was a teacher in another school, not an administrator, so why would anyone mention my name?

The next day I called the school, asked to speak to the department supervisor, and it turned out she was one of my former professors in college. I never asked how or even why she mentioned my name, or how Grace heard, but three months later I was appointed for a position that changed my life, and changed my career from teacher to administrator, a direction I never thought I would take, and if Grace hadn't mentioned this to me over the fence, my life would have taken me on a different path.

There are many veterans in the cemetery, eighty from the Civil War, and many from every war since then—World War I and II, the Korean War, Vietnam—and each grave has a small flag, placed there on Memorial Day and left there all summer. I like fixing the flags that toppled over and replanting the small sticks back beside the gravestones, a small way to honor the flag, the service, and the dead. Local people. Ordinary lives. Extraordinary circumstances.

I just read about the US flag that Neil Armstrong planted on the moon over fifty years ago. I smiled when I read about that flag. NASA is known for its extraordinary technical know-how, for all the extraordinary engineering and hardware that went into the first moon visit, and yet they eventually admitted that the flag they set up on the moon was bought from Sears, the department store chain. I loved that. Just an ordinary flag from an ordinary store, transformed into an extraordinary footnote to history.

We are all extraordinary footnotes to history, making our way to the breakfast table, working during the day, watching a bit of television, planting flowers, visiting friends, loving those we love. Just ordinary, simple lives.

They say that the flag on the moon disintegrated because of the sunlight and the radiation exposure, but Grace doesn't fade in my mind. I remember her smile. I remember her delight as she picked daffodils. I remember how much she loved her three children and her grandchildren.

Carl Sandburg, one of my favorite poets, wrote, "The people will live on. / The learning and blundering people will live on."

I learned how to change diapers for my three children, learned how to paint my house, seed the lawn, and write a few books. I blundered in some relationships and financial decisions, lost friends, my father died, I am often sad, but as Sandburg wrote about us common people, "You can't laugh off their capacity to take it." We all can take it, the struggles and joys if we have the will.

In Shakespeare's *Romeo and Juliet*, Friar Lawrence needed to get a message to Romeo that Juliet will pretend that she is dead, and Romeo was not to worry when he found her. One of Friar Lawrence's colleagues, a humble, simple, ordinary priest, was the messenger. All he had to do was get the message to Romeo, but of course poor Brother John was prevented from traveling with the message because the plague was in town so Romeo, hearing that Juliet was dead, killed himself in grief. The simple, ordinary Friar John never delivered the simple little message.

How often do our lives depend upon ordinary people doing ordinary things? Grace did deliver a message to me about my future. Neil Armstrong, an ordinary man, delivered his historical step onto the moon. What we do with our simple lives is what makes for a community as we contribute our small victories and blunders along the way.

Those of us who live ordinary lives in goodness and who cannot be bought, those of us who live in the fire of our lives in our homes and admire the stars, those of us who cannot be hindered by the wind or by defeat, know that time is a great teacher, that flags from Sears are great symbols, and that Grace was a good neighbor.

"Who," Carl Sandburg wrote, "can't live without hope?"

I can't.

THE WRITER'S VOICE

*What really knocks me out is a book that, when you're all
done reading it, you wish the author that wrote it was a
terrific friend of yours and you could call him up on the phone
whenever you felt like it. That doesn't happen much, though.*
—J. D. SALINGER, *The Catcher in the Rye*

The novelist Toni Morrison died at the age of eighty-eight. I never
met Ms. Morrison. I have read a number of her books, but it
goes way beyond fan remorse that I felt a deep sadness when I
first heard of her loss. In my own small way, I felt a kinship with the
author of *Beloved*, who had one of her characters say, "She is a
friend of my mind. She gather me, man. The pieces I am, she gather
them and give them back to me in all the right order."

I make my own small attempt to gather myself back in the right
order as I write my novels, poems, and essays. Ms. Morrison spent
much of her life in New Jersey, teaching at Princeton University, just
an hour or so drive from where I am.

When I read that Edna St. Vincent Millay tumbled down the
staircase in her home in Austerlitz, New York, and broke her neck, I
wished that I had been there to catch her.

When I read that the poet Sylvia Plath killed herself with the
open gas in her kitchen, I remembered this line from her poem
"Elms": "I have suffered the atrocity of sunsets." I wish Sylvia's

husband hadn't abandoned her. I wish sunsets could have inspired her to hope and love, as she struggled with sorrow and despair.

In the spring of 2018, I was privileged to join Wendell Berry and his wife Tanya for an afternoon visit at their home in Port Royal, Kentucky. I asked if I could come, for I was giving a talk an hour from where he lived, and with his kindness and generosity he said yes. He and I have corresponded for many years. Not only did his poetry inspire me when I was a young man, but also the way he lives his life, as a writer, made me see that a person can survive with his passions, in Wendell's case advocating for the environment, speaking passionately about the disappearance of family farms and a waning rural way of living, and of course writing novels and poetry.

Through my friendship with Wendell, I understood that a writer's life is possible to weave into the ordinary life of earning a living, teaching, mowing the grass, reading the paper. I felt a kinship. Just being in his home, sitting at his kitchen table, taking notice of the sunlight through his windows, I was encouraged.

I said when we parted, "God bless you, Wendell," and he returned the blessing.

Toni Morrison wrote, "Something that is loved is never lost." The books we love, the writers we admire . . . their messages weave in and out of our lives like visiting relatives with a box of taffy. Something memorable. Something never lost.

In a poem I just finished, "The Meaning of Stars," I wrote,

> I once thought the tips of each star were in reach
> If I stood tall enough, felt the lightness of air
> And rose above my own spirit, above my own buoyancy,
> Above the unforgiving earth to free me from its grip."

Writers free us from the grip of our ordinary disappointments and desires. Writers give us buoyancy in our lives to rise above our own spirits and free ourselves as we make our way through the lightness of air and beyond the influence of the rose. Thank you, Toni. Thank you, Wendell.

WAKE UP

I like the dreams of the future better than the history of the past.
—THOMAS JEFFERSON

What did J. D. Salinger, Paul Revere, and Alfred Stieglitz have in common? Yes, they all shared the same birthday: January 1, but they also shared a contribution to the ideals of what America is all about and who we are as a people.

Salinger's famous novel *The Catcher in the Rye* guided an entire generation of Baby Boomers to avoid fake, phony people. Holden Caulfield, a sarcastic, moody, perceptive teenager admitted, "I'm the most terrific liar you ever saw in your life. If I'm on my way to the store to buy a magazine, even, and somebody asks me where I'm going, I'm liable to say I'm going to the opera. It's terrible."

We have built in our contemporary American character the compulsion to lie. We see tobacco, airline, and auto industries lie about health, emissions, and safety. We have politicians who lie about what they believe and what they've done. Banks lie to us about their products. The church lied to us about the sanctity of the clergy. We allow fine print in advertisements and commercials to manipulate the truth about products and prices.

One of Holden's teachers said, "Life is a game, boy. Life is a game that one plays according to the rule."

Holden responds, as so many people today respond, "Yes, sir. I know it is. I know it."

But then Holden says to himself, as we all say to ourselves, "Game, my ass. Some game. If you get on the side where all the hot-shots are, then it's a game, all right—I'll admit that. But if you get on the other side, where there aren't any hot-shots, then what's a game about? Nothing. No game."

Holden said that he left Elkton Hills, a school he detested, because he was surrounded by phonies. Phonies surround all of us.

How do we combat deceit and lies dripping with arrogance? Alfred Steiglitz, one of our premiere pioneers in American photography, said in an exhibition catalogue from the Anderson Galleries in New York in 1921, "I was born in Hoboken. I am an American. Photography is my passion. The search for Truth is my Obsession."

But despite the phonies, despite the ugliness that surrounds us, we have an obsession with truth: all people are created equal, we all have equal rights to life, liberty, and the pursuit of happiness, and whenever these rights are threatened by any form of government, it is the right of the people to alter or to abolish it.

Harvey Fondiller, in *The Best of Popular Photography*, wrote, "Stieglitz was once asked: 'How does a photographer learn?' He answered without a second's hesitation: 'By looking.'"

It is no surprise that Stieglitz married the artist Georgia O'Keeffe, who said, "If you take a flower in your hand and really look at it, it's your world for a moment."

What is our American world at the moment? How closely are we looking at the suffering of immigrants? How closely are we looking at the environment? How closely are we looking at our health, our liberties, and our happiness in the face of the pursuit of the dollar bill? How closely are we looking at the world's hunger and slaughter of the innocent? We learn by looking.

Paul Revere became famous for looking over his shoulder as he furiously rode to Concord, Massachusetts, in April 1775 to warn the citizens that the British soldiers were on their way for battle. Poet Henry Wadsworth Longfellow made that ride famous as he described Revere's cry of defiance, his fearless voice in the darkness, his knocking on doors and how throughout our history we in America still hear in hours of darkness and peril the midnight cry, "Our freedom is threatened! A despot on a throne is attempting to destroy who we are as a people! Wake up! Look closely! Wake up!"

I hope that we will wake up and listen to that cry.

THE ILLUSIONS OF WAR

I know not with what weapons World War III will be fought,
but World War IV will be fought with sticks and stones.
—ALBERT EINSTEIN

Behind the house where I grew up was an abandoned garbage pit: bottles, rotting shoes, rusted tin cans. It was a place my sisters and brothers and I used for our treasure hunts and sometimes we were lucky: marbles, a 1909 car license plate, and our biggest find: an enamel leg of a kitchen sink that looked like a long, yellow machine gun.

One summer afternoon as we and the neighborhood kids were reenacting World War I, I dragged my yellow monster of a gun, propped it on the rocks near the rosebushes in the backyard, and starting "shooting" at my brother as he jumped behind the apple tree. That is when my grandfather stood up from his lawn chair, stood above me in his white shorts and cotton shirt, and asked, sadly, that I stop, and then he walked away.

I didn't understand as a child that the fantasy of war is a dangerous mechanism that reduces the horrors of people killing each other.

On December 23, 1915, my grandfather, a volunteer in the Belgian army, was critically shot in his left arm in Dixmude, Belgium, in the Trenches of Death.

The invading German forces were determined to crash through Belgium and overtake the French ports of Calais and Dunkirk but were stopped because of the trenches in Dixmude, and because of the extraordinary resilience and sacrifices the Belgian forces and my grandfather made holding back the enemy for four years.

My grandfather spent over a year in the hospital enduring operation after operation in an attempt to save his arm. In the end his left arm was a useless appendage, like a thick rope hanging down from his shoulder. During the Second World War my grandfather, as a director of communications, was on the front lines as the Nazis invaded Belgium on May 10, 1940.

My grandfather, Major General Joseph Henri Kestens, at the end of the Second World War, was awarded the Croix de Guerre for bravery, and he served in the army as part of the Belgian Resistance before being captured and imprisoned in Spain. Following his liberation, he spent the rest of the war in London, where General Montgomery, Charles de Gaulle, and Dwight Eisenhower all issued personal commendations to my grandfather for his bravery and service.

I am 68 years old. My wife and I have been married for 42 years. We have three adult children and one grandchild, Finnian. If, on December 23, 1915, that enemy bullet that shattered my grandfather's arm was aimed six inches to the left, one-year-old Finnian would not have been building blocks with me on the carpet last night as he laughed and laughed.

It is estimated that over 37 million civilians and soldiers people died during World War I, and more than 60 million during World

War II. How many people were never born? How many lives destroyed? How much sorrow unleashed?

I felt powerful lugging my kitchen sink machine gun around the yard when I was a boy. At the time I did not understand the sorrow in my grandfather's face as he walked away and sat back onto the lawn chair and opened his newspaper.

CAN YOU SEE?

Thou hast seen nothing yet.
—MIGUEL DE CERVANTES, *Don Quixote*

I didn't sleep well last night, so I walked downstairs and sat on the couch with my cat, Stuart, on my lap. He was happy of course, purring, enjoying the caresses on his head and under his chin, but then he jumped off and stood beside the door wanting to go out.

I stood up and turned the knob of the back door, and as Stuart ran out onto the deck, I followed. Stuart is a black cat, so he immediately disappeared into the darkness, and I looked up into the slate sky. Living so close to New York City and being in the heart of the New York suburbs, I do not see many stars.

My parents bought a small piece of property over sixty years ago in Ontario, Canada, and built a small cabin just off a dirt road. There the stars look like a king's treasure: the brilliance of Venus, the explosion of the Milky Way, the quick diamond necklace of shooting stars.

Star light, star bright,
First star I see tonight;
Wish I may, wish I might,
Have the wish I wish tonight.

No one knows who wrote this famous nursery rhyme: not Copernicus, who studied our most powerful star and realized the earth revolves around the sun. Jiminy Cricket might have written it if he was a real person and not an animated creature crooning about wishing upon a star in *Pinocchio*.

Hooking ourselves to the stars at night can remind us that there is stability in the universe. Those stars, like notes in a score by Beethoven, have been there for millions of years, and will continue to be there millions of years into the future long after we die.

I stood on the deck and was able to see the Big Dipper to my left. The single streetlamp down the road cast a yellow light at the hem of the maple tree.

Vincent Van Gogh, during his stay in an institution following his great depression, created one of his most famous paintings, *Starry Night*. Soon after he completed the work, Vincent wrote to his brother Theo, "This morning I saw the countryside from my window a long time before sunrise with nothing but the morning star which looked very big." That star was probably Venus, and that painting is probably his finest. Vincent wrote that "we take death to each star."

We send up ourselves to the puzzlement of nature, with the limitations of our lives while the stars have the arrogance to exist for eons. But Van Gogh, like us, grappled with the magnificent struggle. He also said: "I find a tremendous need for, shall I say the word—for religion—so I go outside to paint the stars."

If you look at Van Gogh's *Starry Night* you will see, like us, a village at rest, or that appears to be at rest with its lit windows and brown roof tops. Van Gogh drew quiet lines and squares in repose perhaps ready for an intruder, or a silent partner, we who come to his painting seeking a stable community within ourselves. But if you look above the placid village there is the spectacle of swirls, the energy of the sky, the power of the moon and the aggressive cypress tree. The contrast between the sleeping village and the turbulent night suggests our own spiritual chaos, grappling with the balance between our spiritual and mortal selves.

Sylvia Plath had it right when she wrote in her poem "Stars Over the Dordogne," "And where I lie now, back in my own dark star, / I see those constellations in my head."

We have swirling in our minds starry nights, confusion, depression, sorrows, things that keep us up in the night. Plath said in her poem that she is "unwarmed by the sweet air of this peach orchard." So, what does give us solace? What does bring warmth and comfort to us when we are lost and afraid? Sylvia wrote, "I shut my eyes / And drink the small night chill like news of home."

Wish I may, wish I might have the wish I wish tonight. Stuart stepped out of the darkness and rubbed himself against my legs. I picked up the cat, waltzed with him a bit on the deck, looked up at the stars one more time, and then stepped back into the house, and I was home.

LOOK CLOSELY

When you're at the end of your rope, tie a knot and hold on.
—THEODORE ROOSEVELT

Someone once said to me that if we want to see a true reflection of who we are, place those people we love in a semicircle in front of us, and there we have a true mirror.

In Greek mythology, the handsome hunter Narcissus loved his own looks so much that when we saw himself in the reflection of a pool, he could not tear himself away. He looked and preened and admired himself for so long that he could not bear to live any longer, and so he died. We look in the mirror to fix our hair, to straighten a tie, or to ask if we are beautiful, as the Evil Queen asked so often to her magic mirror.

When photons (rays of light) reflect from our faces and hit a smooth surface of a mirror, those photons bounce back and the eyes pick our images, but in reverse.

What do we see in the mirror of history? We often hear in the cliché that we need to learn about history so that we don't make the same mistakes.

I recently visited Hildene, Robert Lincoln's house in Manchester, Vermont. This was the home of Abraham Lincoln's only child to survive into adulthood. William Lincoln died at the age of twelve from typhoid. Tad Lincoln was eighteen when he died of what some historians believe to have been pneumonia. And, tragically,

Edward Lincoln was only four when he died of what some thought was cancer. Mary Todd Lincoln, Abraham's wife, suffered deep depression for the rest of her life as she tried to endure the tragic deaths of her children and husband.

Robert Lincoln built the Georgian Revival mansion in 1905, and today it stands as a testimony to Robert's success as a lawyer, Secretary of War, and CEO of the Pullman Car Company. He did not seek the limelight, he raised his family, and lived an admirable life.

On the second floor of the mansion, the Friends of Hildene foundation built a small section with artifacts belonging to Robert's father. There you will see letters the president wrote. In a glass display case is Lincoln's famous stovepipe hat and above the hat is a mirror that was in the president's White House residence. It is believed that Abraham checked his appearance in this mirror before joining his wife for an evening's entertainment at Ford Theater.

As I stood before this oval mirror and saw my reflection, I thought about the president adjusting his tie, or smoothing out his jacket. When we look into the eyes of ourselves, what do we see? When we look into the eyes of history what do we see?

Lincoln famously said in a speech in 1856:

You can fool all the people some of the time, and some of the people all of the time, but you cannot fool all the people all of the time.

A fool can tell us that he is a genius, that he is stable and extraordinary. Some people will believe him for a short time. A narcissist often has an engaging personality and exhibits a bluster that is hard to avoid and easy to envy for a time. But then the power of delusion begins to diminish, and the façade fades.

"Mirror, mirror on the wall, who is the fairest of them all?" The photons of light that are reflected from the face of a charlatan begin to reflect back to us in reverse and we see the upside-down image of a false reality.

I looked into Abraham Lincoln's mirror and I could hear his words: "I have always found than mercy bears richer fruits that strict justice." And these: "Love is the chain to lock a child to its parents." And: "Truth is your truest friend, no matter what the circumstances are." And, "It really hurts me very much to suppose that I have wronged anybody on earth."

If we place in a semicircle before us all the presidents we have elected in our country, we will see a pretty good reflection of who we are as a people: admirable and despicable; intelligent and dull; honorable and deceitful; selfless and selfish; humble and arrogant; generous and greedy. I believe that every newly elected president ought to arrive at the White House with his or her own polished mirror.

AFFIRMATIVE

I am a yea-sayer.

—FRIEDRICH NIETZSCHE

It is 5:00 in the morning and I hear the sound of a distant train. Do you live close enough to a train passing through your town? Why is it that when we hear the distant whistle we feel a longing, or a loneliness? Do we wish for an adventure with Tintin and Snowy to the Himalayas?

I grew up with Tintin, the Belgian reporter who traveled the world with his dog, Snowy. My parents brought the French children's books with them from Belgium, and when I discovered the books on the shelf as a boy I followed each page as if I was Tintin's most trusted partner.

Tintin began as a comic strip in the Belgian newspaper *Le Soir*, created by Georges Remi who used the pen name Hergé. Because I could not read French, I used my imagination to determine what the characters were saying.

Tintin visited Egypt, China, the United States, and Tibet. He sailed with Captain Haddock on his freighter, hid in a Chinese vase, rode camels, and floated above the earth in an orange space suit. My friends had Dick Tracy and Superman; I had Tintin. I *was* Tintin.

I felt like jumping up from my desk this morning. I felt like running out of the house toward the train and calling out "Come on, Tintin! Come on, Snowy! Another adventure!"

Silence, except for the ringing in my ears.

Now I hear the sound of a jet plane. I live under the incoming flight patterns of planes landing at Newark International Airport, but because I live forty-five minutes from the airport, the distant roar of the jets is a pleasing reminder that activity is taking place outside my window, that people are on their way, that the world is in motion. I often take my binoculars and stand on the deck to see what airline is flying over the house: Delta, United, Southwest.

When I was a teenager one of our neighbors was a pilot for United Airlines, so I asked him one day what it took to be a pilot. He invited me to his house where he gave me a glossy brochure on the company. He spoke about college, the Air Force, flight training, and then he said the cursed word: math. He said that pilots use calculus and algebra all the time, and they need deep understanding of geometry. So I knew for sure that Tintin was never going to be a pilot for United Airlines.

I was fifteen years old the first time I flew in an airplane. My godfather, one of my parents' closest friends, was going to be installed as an archbishop in the Byzantine Church in Alabama. My father was going to the ceremony and asked me if I'd like to go. I was thrilled to sit near the window and look out as we flew over the landscape and clouds. I was horrified when we landed because I saw signs in bold letters: "Colored Waiting Room," "Laundry Company: We Wash for White People Only." "We Serve Colored: Carry out only."

Silence, except for the ringing in my ears.

I had a hearing test two years ago and the doctor said that at my age ringing in the ear is not uncommon and that there is nothing that can be done to make it stop. The ambient noise of the day masks the annoyance, but when I go to bed, there it is. I am fortunate in a way because the ringing sound is similar to the night sounds of the summer outside my window, which I find soothing, and so when I am in bed, I imagine the hum and gentle noise rolling in my ears is the symphony of crickets and tree frogs, and then I sleep.

Mothers die. Racism is a curse on humanity. Boys can't fly without geometry. I am not Tintin.

Silence, except for the ringing in my ears.

BALM TO OUR SOULS

The music of the spinning wheel will be as a balm to your souls.
—MAHATMA GANDHI

When my father was a young man he built his own weaving loom, bought a spinning wheel, spun his own wool to make his own thread, and designed his own patterns for the loom.

I can still hear in my memory the sound of the click-clack of the loom as my father made shawls, wall hangings, and scarves. My father was an editor, writer, and lawyer. He loved to fiddle with architecture; he translated religious texts from Greek to English; and he loved his loom. After a while he no longer spun his own wool. Instead, he bought balls of yarn and abandoned the spinning wheel and relegated it to the corner of the attic.

As a boy, I discovered the spinning wheel and used it many, many times as the steering wheel of my pirate galleon. I would also push the pedal and see how fast I could spin the wheel before it would jump off its track and crash to the floor.

The spinning wheel rattled and shook. I liked taking it apart just for fun and reassembling it. The wheel broke. (Maybe I broke it.) I grew up. No one in my family took any interest in spinning and the wheel again sat in the attic for over forty years.

Yesterday my son David and my daughter-in-law Emily invited Roe and me for brunch. Emily made delicious Eggs Benedict over crab cakes, and for dessert she served a dish of sweet, succulent blackberries. Elegant. Generous. Great fun. After brunch, Emily said, "I have news to share." David smiled.

Emily left the dining room and returned with my father's spinning wheel. My mother had given it to Emily and David because they had discovered the creative joy of knitting, so much so that they wanted to learn how to spin their own wool, and when I mentioned this to my mother, she was pleased to give the spinning wheel to my children.

David and Emily were able to find a woodworker who specialized in spinning wheels, and this clever man fixed the broken wheel, carved new bobbins and spindles, and was able to return it to its full function. However, after a while, it didn't seem to work so well, so David and Emily bought a modern spinning wheel that worked out just fine. It seemed that the old wheel was going to be banished again, doomed to being a decoration in the corner of a room.

"I have good news to share," Emily said as she poured me a delicious, warm cup of apple cider. "I have mastered Papa's spinning wheel and learned its value. I can spin a thin thread, much thinner than on the new wheel, and I find the thin thread to be so much better for knitting." Then Emily gave a demonstration. She pulled a strand of wool from a cleaned fleece and with dexterity, skill, and contentment she began spinning the wool into a lovely off-white thread.

Both David and Emily were thrilled to learn the value of my father's spinning wheel, and how well it works. David wanted to know my memories of my father spinning. He likes the idea that Emily is using the same apparatus my father used so many years ago.

In Mahatma Gandhi's publication *Harijan*, he wrote, "The music of the spinning wheel will be as a balm to your souls."

Watching Emily spin is like watching the confident world at peace creating beauty moment by moment as the singing wheel turns and the thread twirls happily around the rotating bobbin.

My father would have been pleased.

CONCLUSION
THINGS THAT MATTER MOST

Time ran out. My mother was ravished with arthritis, often tired, but always filled with optimism and joy.

She read *The Guardian*, the *New Yorker*, the *Atlantic Monthly*, the *New York Times*. She was an author of many books.

My mother continued to write every day. She had just finished reading *Wild Swans: Three Daughters of China*, the extraordinary novel written by Jung Chang.

Time ran out. My mother was 99 years old and said one afternoon a few months ago, "Always keep in mind the secret name of beauty."

My mother remembered that a few hours before I was born she was baking a peach pie. She was my first teacher: introducing me to the color of the autumn leaves, and reading aloud Beatrix Potter's *The Tale of Peter Rabbit*. We collected wildflowers together in the spring. In grade school my mother gave me Kenneth Grahame's book *The Wind in the Willows*. In middle school my mother placed on my pillow Sterling North's *Rascal*, a book about that mischievous raccoon. In high school she introduced me to the books of Loren Eiseley and William Carlos Williams. When I met a girl, my mother gave me her engagement ring to pass along to the woman who has now been my wife for 45 years.

My mother endured Nazi occupation in Belgium for four years, nearly died in Dunkirk bombing raids, raised six children here in

America . . . including my brother Oliver, who was born with no intellect, was blind, mute, unable to chew.

Time ran out.

"Day by day, we cross over into the future," my mother wrote in a poem. My mother is buried beside my father and brother Oliver in a small Benedictine cemetery in Weston, Vermont.

When I visited my mother at the house where I grew up, we sometimes sat on the terrace just outside her bedroom. In spring the wisteria dripped those beautiful purple flowers. In the fall the green leaves protected us. Often a chipmunk joined us on the terrace as my mother and I reminisced about weddings, vacations, and peach pie.

"This terrace is a fragment of paradise," my mother said as the brave chipmunk scurried up beside her chair. As she leaned over, the chipmunk sat up and gently took the peanut from my mother's hand. A blue jay swooped down from the pine tree and grabbed a peanut that my mother had tossed onto the terrace floor.

We laughed at the quick chipmunk. We talked about the sorrows in the news and about the deer she saw sleeping in the yard at the edge of the woods. We even spoke about God.

"Isn't it lovely that we are here, at ease, loving the world?"

We are living in a world that is being ravaged with war, fires, and hurricanes, political upheavals, hunger, violence that is loose upon the world. It has always been so. But these things are news because they are stains that attempt to mar the beauty of our souls, my mother would say. Goodness isn't news because it is so common.

On the terrace, as my mother fed her chipmunk, she looked up at me and said, "You don't think of it, Christopher, but far ahead, yet closer than a heartbeat, something immense, wild, holy grabs you and won't let go."

Yes, time ran out. My mother's heart gave up in December. Flowers perish, trees shed their leaves, and fields shrivel into brown stalks and frozen earth.

As my mother and I slowly walked back into her bedroom, and as we took our last steps off the terrace arm in arm she looked up and said, "We can always return to a life of simplicity and peace."

My mother was 99 years old and time ran out. She saw my sadness and then with a sigh and a smile, as she struggled back into her bedroom chair, she whispered, "Christopher, we do not die forever."

On a Sunday my mother had a severe heart attack. On Monday we spoke as she propped herself up in the hospital bed. "I am going home tomorrow," she said confidently.

We spoke on the phone about her great-grandchildren, Finnian and Indigo. She said how kind and gentle the doctors and nurses were. Her last words to me before we hung up were, "I love you, Christopher." Her last words to me.

Two days later my mother died peacefully.

We live in fragments of paradise. Lucky are we who recognize what matters most: the fireflies of love . . . always love, always love, always love.

Kyrie eleison.

SOURCES

Andersen, Hans. *Fairy Tales*. London: Frederick Warne and Co., 1890.

Baldwin, James. *The Fire Next Time*. New York: Dial Press, 1963.

Barrie, J. M. *Peter and Wendy*. London, Hodder & Stoughton, 1911.

Barth, John. *Sabbatical*. New York: Putnam Publishing Group, 1982.

Blixen, Karen. *Out of Africa*. New York: Putnam, 1937.

Bradbury, Ray. *Fahrenheit 451*. New York: Ballantine Books, 1963.

Carroll, Lewis. *Through the Looking Glass*. New York: Macmillan, 1872.

———. *Alice's Adventures in Wonderland*. New York: Macmillan, 1865.

Chase, Mary. *Harvey*. New York: Dramatists Plays Service, 1951.

Dahl, Roald, *Minpins*. New York: Puffin Books, 2009.

de Chardin, Pierre Teilhard. *The Phenomenon of Man*. New York: Harper & Brothers, 1959.

de Saint-Exupéry, Antoine. *The Little Prince*. New York: Reynal & Hitchcock, 1943.

Dickens, Charles. *A Christmas Carol*. London: Chapman and Hall, 1843.

Doyle, Arthur Conan. *A Study in Scarlet*. London: Ward & Lock Co., 1887.

Einstein, Albert. *The Special Theory of Relativity*. New York: George Braziller, 1912.

Eliot, George. *Middlemarch*. Edinburgh: William Blackwood & Sons, 1871.

Fassler, Joe. *Light the Dark: Writers on Creativity, Inspiration and the Artistic Process*. New York: Penguin Books, 2017.

Fitzgerald, F. Scott. *The Great Gatsby*. New York: Charles Scribner's Sons, 1925.

Fondiller, Harvey. *The Best of Popular Photography*. New York: Watson-Guptill Publishers, 1980.

Frank, Anne. *The Diary of a Young Girl*. New York: Bantam, 1993.

Frost, Robert. *North of Boston*. New York: Holt, 1915.

Grant, Ulysses. *Personal Memoirs of Ulysses S. Grant*. New York: Charles L. Webster and Company, 1885.

Hemingway, Ernest. *The Old Man and the Sea*. New York: Charles Scribner's & Sons, 1952.

Kawabata, Yasunari, *Snow Country*. New York: Vintage, 1996.

Keats, John, *The Poetical Works of John Keats*, Oxford: Oxford University Press, 1929.

Kennedy, John Fitzgerald. *Public Papers of the Presidents of the United States: John F. Kennedy*, 1963.

Kundera, Milan. *The Unbearable Lightness of Being*. New York: Harper & Row, 1984.

Lamott, Anne. *Bird by Bird*. New York: Anchor, 1995.

Leach, Jim. *Wendell Berry, Landsman*. *Humanities*: The Magazine of the National Endowment for the Humanities. May/June 2012.

Lee, Harper. *To Kill a Mockingbird*. New York: J.B. Lippincott & Co., 1960.

Lindbergh, Anne Morrow. *Gift from the Sea*. New York: Pantheon Books, 1955.

London, Jack. *Getting into Print*. New York: The Editor, 1903.

Merton, Thomas. *Conjectures of a Guilty Bystander*. London: Burns & Oates, 1968.

Morrison, Toni. *Beloved*. New York: Alfred A. Knopf, 1987.

Neruda, Pablo. *Twenty Love Poems and a Sing of Despair*. San Francisco: Chronicle Books, 1993.

Nouwen, Henri. *Can You Drink this Cup?*. Notre Dame, IN: Ave Maria Press, 1996.

Obama, Barrack. *Dreams of My Father*. New York: Three Rivers Press, 2004.

Octavio Paz, *Collected Poems of Octavio Paz*. New York: New Directions, 1991.

Plath, Sylvia. *The Collected Poems*. New York: Harper Perennial Modern Classics, 2018.

Poe, Edgar Allen. *The Tell-Tale Heart*. New York: The Pioneer, 1843.

Potter, Beatrix. *Mrs. Tiggy-Winkle*. London: Frederick Warne & Co., 1905.

Rilke, Rainer Maria. *Letters of Cezanne*. Los Angeles: J. Paul Getty Museum, 2013.

———. *Letters to a Young Poet*. New York: Penguin, 2014.

Roth, Philip. *Portnoy's Complaint*. New York: Random House, 1969.

Salinger, J. D. *The Catcher in the Rye*. New York: Little Brown, 1951.

Sandburg, Carl. *Yes, the People*. New York: Harcourt, Brace and Company, 1936.

Sarton, May. *Mrs. Stevens Hears the Mermaids Singing*. New York: W.W. Norton & Company, 1965.

Sendak, Maurice. *Where the Wild Things Are*. New York: Harper, 1963.

Shaw, George Bernard. *Pygmalion*. New York: Brentano, 1916.

Shelly, Mary, *Frankenstein*. London: Lackington, Hughes, Harding, Mavor & Jones, 1818.

Simon, Paul, *The Sound of Silence*. Santa Monica, CA: © Universal Music
Publishing Group, 1964.

Stegner, Wallace. *Angel of Repose*. New York: Doubleday, 1971.

——. *On Teaching and Writing Fiction*. New York: Penguin, 2002.

Teasdale, Sara. *Collected Poems*. New York: Buccaneer Books, 1996.

Thomas, Dylan. *A Child's Christmas in Wales*. New York: New Directions,
1995.

Thoreau, Henry David. *Walden*. Boston: Ticknor and Fields, 1854.

Tolkien, J. R. R. *The Hobbit, or There and Back Again*. Sydney: Allen and
Unwin, 1937.

Travers, P. L. *Mary Poppins*. London: Gerald Howe Ltd., 1934.

Twain, Mark. *The Adventures of Tom Sawyer*. New York: The American
Publishing Company, 1876.

Wiesel, Elie. *Night*. New York: Hill and Yang, 2006.

Wilder, Thornton. *The Skin of Our Teeth*. New York: Harper & Brothers,
1942.

——. *Our Town*. New York. Harper Perennial Modern Classics, 2003.

Williams, William Carlos. *The Collected Earlier Poems*. New York: New
Directions, 1966.

Wolfe, Thomas. *You Can't Go Home Again*. New York: Harper & Row,
1940.

——. *Look Homeward, Angel*. New York: Charles Scribner's and Sons,
1929.

Woolf, Virginia. *Jacob's Room*. London: Hogarth Press, 1922.

ABOUT PARACLETE PRESS

PARACLETE PRESS is the publishing arm of the
Cape Cod Benedictine community, the Community
of Jesus. Presenting a full expression of Christian
belief and practice, we reflect the ecumenical
charism of the Community and its dedication to
sacred music, the fine arts, and the written word.

Learn more about us at our website:

*SCAN
TO READ*

www.paracletepress.com